Praise for the Chocoholic Mysteries

The Chocolate Frog Frame-Up

"A JoAnna Carl mystery will be a winner. The trivia and vivid descriptions of the luscious confections are enough to make you hunger for more"
—Roundtable Reviews

"Delicious." —Cluesunlimited

"A fast-paced, light read, full of chocolate facts and delectable treats. Lee is an endearing heroine. . . . Readers will enjoy the time they spend with Lee and Joe in Warner Pier and will look forward to returning for more murder dipped in chocolate."
—The Mystery Reader

"The descriptions of the chocolates are enough to make your mouth water, so be prepared. . . . Once again, I enjoyed each page of the book and am already looking forward to my next visit to Warner Pier, Michigan." —Review Index

continued . . .

The Chocolate Bear Burglary

"Do not read *The Chocolate Bear Burglary* on an empty stomach because the luscious . . . descriptions of exotic chocolate will have you running out to buy gourmet sweets. . . . A delectable treat." —*Midwest Book Review*

"[Carl] teases with descriptions of mouthwatering bonbons and truffles while she drops clues. . . . [Lee is] vulnerable and real, endearingly defective. . . . Fast-paced and sprinkled with humor. Strongly recommended." —I Love a Mystery

"Kept me entertained to the very last word! . . . A great new sleuth . . . interesting facts about chocolate. . . . A delicious new series." —*Romantic Times*

The Chocolate Cat Caper

"A mouthwatering debut and a delicious new series! Feisty young heroine Lee McKinney is a delight in this chocolate treat. A real page-turner, and I got chocolate on every one! I can't wait for the next."
—Tamar Myers

"As delectable as a rich chocolate truffle, and the mystery filling satisfies to the last prized morsel. Lee McKinney sells chocolates and solves crimes with panache and good humor. More, please. And I'll take one of those dark chocolate oval bonbons."   —Carolyn Hart

"One will gain weight just from reading [this]. . . . Delicious. . . . The beginning of what looks like a terrific new cozy series."   —*Midwest Book Review*

"Enjoyable . . . entertaining . . . a fast-paced whodunit with lots of suspects and plenty of surprises . . . satisfies a passion for anything chocolate. In the fine tradition of Diane Mott Davidson."   —*The Commercial Record*

Also by JoAnna Carl

The Chocolate Cat Caper
The Chocolate Bear Burglary
The Chocolate Frog Frame-Up

The Chocolate Puppy Puzzle

A Chocoholic Mystery

JoAnna Carl

A SIGNET BOOK

SIGNET
Published by New American Library, a division of
Penguin Group (USA) Inc., 375 Hudson Street,
New York, New York 10014, USA
Penguin Group (Canada), 10 Alcorn Avenue, Toronto,
Ontario M4V 3B2, Canada (a division of Pearson Penguin Canada Inc.)
Penguin Books Ltd., 80 Strand, London WC2R 0RL, England
Penguin Ireland, 25 St. Stephen's Green, Dublin 2,
Ireland (a division of Penguin Books Ltd.)
Penguin Group (Australia), 250 Camberwell Road, Camberwell, Victoria 3124,
Australia (a division of Pearson Australia Group Pty. Ltd.)
Penguin Books India Pvt. Ltd., 11 Community Centre, Panchsheel Park,
New Delhi - 110 017, India
Penguin Group (NZ), Cnr Airborne and Rosedale Roads, Albany,
Auckland 1310, New Zealand (a division of Pearson New Zealand Ltd.)
Penguin Books (South Africa) (Pty.) Ltd., 24 Sturdee Avenue,
Rosebank, Johannesburg 2196, South Africa

Penguin Books Ltd., Registered Offices:
80 Strand, London WC2R 0RL, England

First published by Signet, an imprint of New American Library,
a division of Penguin Group (USA) Inc.

First Printing, December 2004
10 9 8 7 6 5 4 3 2 1

For Norma Hightower,
a special cousin and friend

Acknowledgments

As ever, I exploited numerous friends and relatives as I wrote this book. Of particular help were the wonderful; folks at Morgen Chocolate Incorporated in Dallas, including Rex Morgan, Betsy Peters, and Andrea Pedraza. Michigan friends helped; Susan McDermott, who goes far beyond mere neighborliness in answering questions; Tracy Paquin, who grew up on a fruit farm and was willing to tell me about it; and their golden retriever, Mitchell. Thanks also go to Janet Lockwood, of the Michigan Film Office, a true public servant; to Jack Slaybaugh, a kind coin and money collector; to expert dog trainer Helen Smith; and to my brother, Kim Kimbrell.

Acknowledgments

Chapter 1

I suppose it wasn't the puppy's fault, but after he handed me the money, everything in Warner Pier seemed to go to pot. Fraud, kidnapping, homicide, theft, trespassing—a real crime wave developed. My romantic life got—well, unromantic. Even the chocolate business became complicated.

The day had started out very well. I was happy as I walked toward the Fall Rinkydink. My favorite guy, Joe Woodyard, was with me. The weather was as perfect as only an October day on the shores of Lake Michigan can be. I may have hummed a hum or skipped a little skip.

Then a chocolate Labrador pup galumped across the Dock Street Park, cut through the buffet line in the picnic shelter, and planted two gigantic feet on the knees of my brand-new tan wool slacks. I nearly dropped a big tray of TenHuis Chocolade's finest truffles and bonbons. The sweets all shifted to one side, and only the extra-strength industrial plastic wrap kept them from hitting the grass.

The dog handed me a large leather wallet with a dirty ten-dollar bill sticking out one side.

That first disaster occurred at the first-ever Rinky-dink.

I'm business manager for my aunt's chocolate shop, TenHuis Chocolade, in the picturesque resort of Warner Pier, on the east shore of Lake Michigan. In the summer, Warner Pier's streets—laid out in 1855 for buggies and horse-drawn farm wagons—are thronged with cars, vans, and buses carrying tourists and summer people. The traffic is horrendous.

In the fall, all the tourists and summer visitors go home. The parking problem is over until the next Memorial Day, and traffic is close to nil for six months. Consequently, Warner Pier locals for years have linked the end of the tourist season and the beginning of autumn to the day when our one traffic light becomes a blinker.

All summer the light at Fourth Avenue and Dock Street changes from green to yellow to red—just like a big city traffic light. On the Tuesday after Columbus Day, the Warner Pier Street Department turns out in force (all three of them) and changes the light to a flashing red on Fourth Avenue and a flashing yellow on Dock Street. For years the merchants in the neighborhood gathered to cheer them on, just as a joke.

It was Maggie McNutt, a close friend of mine and Warner Pier High School speech and drama teacher, who had the idea of making the changing of the traffic light into a fund-raiser for the high school drama club. All the food-related merchants, including Ten-Huis (it rhymes with "ice"), were asked to donate food for a picnic luncheon, which would be held in the Dock Street Park picnic shelter. Nonfood merchants—the gift shops, antique stores, and art galleries, the hardware store, and the drug store—were asked to kick in items for a silent auction and for door prizes. Everybody in the world was asked to buy tickets.

"It'll be fun!" said Maggie. She had bounced in her chair as she presented the idea to the chamber board. "The chamber ought to have more social events. This one will be a farewell party for those merchants who close up and go south for the winter. It'll be a celebrate-fall party for those of us staying here. And it will help the drama club take students to state competition."

Maggie had become the speech and drama teacher three years earlier, when she and her husband, Ken, who taught math, were both hired at Warner Pier High School. She had short dark hair and was petite, peppy, and cute—the kind of woman who makes an all-but-six-foot blonde like me feel like a giraffe. But I liked Maggie. Everyone in Warner Pier seemed to like her—with one exception—and Maggie was full of ideas to promote Warner Pier High School drama. Maggie told me she had worked in Hollywood, appearing as an extra in small roles in several films. But when she'd turned thirty, she'd decided she was never going to make it big in show biz, so she came back to her home state, got her master's in education, and married Ken McNutt, who'd been a high school classmate. They'd rented a little house in Warner Pier and settled into the community. The previous year her students had taken first place in the state one-act competition. She wanted to make sure they got to go again.

The name of the event, the "Rinkydink," had started as a joke, after somebody remarked that a town with only one traffic light was "pretty rinky-dink." Since the small-town atmosphere was what most of us liked about living in Warner Pier, we adopted the term with perverse pride, and the light-changing ceremony was officially christened.

The weather was cooperating for the first Rinky-dink, and Maggie hadn't had to move the picnic to the high school gym, as she'd feared she might. The day was sunny, with temperatures just under seventy. The sunlight was creating that autumn effect when oblique light turns the sky mellow and the air so soft and beautiful you want to gulp big lungfuls of it. The trees were lush with all the reds, yellows, golds, oranges, greens, and browns of a Michigan autumn. The sun glinted off the Warner River. The Victorian houses looked more like wedding cakes than usual. The chrysanthemums were blooming like crazy—bronze, maroon, yellow, rust, and gold. The breeze playfully tossed fallen leaves about.

It was a good day to be alive and living in Warner Pier, Michigan. I had been happy as a clam as Joe and I each carried a big tray of TenHuis's fanciest chocolates toward the dessert table.

Joe saw the dog coming. "There's a pup loose," he said. "Some guy is after him."

I turned to see who was chasing the dog. The animal ran right up to me and, as I said, planted his huge puppy feet on the knees of my tan wool slacks. He looked at me with soft hazel eyes. He was holding this big leather wallet in his mouth.

"Hey, fellow! Welcome to the party." I stepped backward, trying to get the dirty feet off my slacks. Of course, the puppy thought this was a game and jumped up on me again. I balanced the tray on my hip, accidentally tipping it. I could feel the chocolates slide as I tried to fend the pup off with the hand I'd freed up. The dog was at that awkward stage of puppyhood, maybe four or five months old. He looked healthy and full of puppy pep, with a lustrous, dark brown coat as smooth and shiny as melted chocolate. He had a tiny spot of white on his chest.

Then the pup nudged my wrist with the wallet. It was a beat-up and moldy-looking brown leather folder, more than twice the size of a standard bifold billfold and more like a passport case than a regular wallet. It didn't look like something a puppy should be chewing on, so I took it away from him. It was covered with dog slobber, of course.

By then Joe had put down the tray of chocolates that he was carrying, and he grabbed the dog.

"Look at the money," I said, showing him the wallet. Five or six odd-sized bills were sticking out. "Somebody's been playing king-sized Monopoly."

"I've seen those big bills in one of the antique shops," Joe said. "I think they used to be legal tender."

"Somebody's going to want this back."

Joe scooped the puppy up with both arms, and the dog joyously licked his face. Joe laughed. What else can you do when a strange puppy decides you're adorable? Or maybe delicious. Of course, I think Joe's delicious, too. He not only has dark hair, brilliant blue eyes, and broad shoulders, he also has a very sharp mind and a nice personality. Someday I might even set a wedding date.

I took my tray of chocolates to the dessert table and handed them to Tracy Roderick, who was a Ten-Huis employee in the summer and president of Maggie McNutt's drama club during the school year. Tracy's a nice girl; she could even be a pretty girl if she got a decent hairstyle.

"Hi, Lee," Tracy said. "I'm in charge of the dessert table. As usual, the TenHuis chocolates will be the center of attraction."

"I messed these up," I said. "They nearly landed in the grass."

Tracy brandished a pair of food-service gloves. "I'll straighten them. Your aunt will never know what a narrow escape they had."

The two of us admired the craftsmanship displayed in the chocolates. Swirling patterns of bon-

bons and truffles filled the two trays, ready to entice
Rinkydink picnickers with dark, white, and milk
chocolate, each goody filled with an exotic flavor. In
the center of each tray was a heap of molded
chocolates—squares, small animals, miniature bars.
Joe and I had just delivered two big trays of yummy.
To me the chocolates made the cherry pies and coffee
cakes a waste of calories.

"Lee, we'd better get this dog back to his owner,"
Joe said.

Leaving Tracy in charge of her desserts, I fished a
large paper napkin out of a pile at the end of the
serving table and wiped off my hand and the wallet.
Then Joe and I walked toward the man who had
been running. He'd slowed down after he saw Joe
scoop up the puppy.

I waved the wallet. "This yours?"

"Thanks for rescuing it!" The man continued
toward us. "And thanks for grabbing Monte!"

As the man approached, I had plenty of time to
look him over. He was an older gent, but he was
marching along as if he were full of youthful energy.
He was wearing an outfit that was just a little too
slickly coordinated—neatly pressed jeans, desert
boots, and a plaid wool shirt worn over a turtleneck.
Gray hair oozed out from beneath a wide-brimmed
felt hat that looked—well, Australian. It didn't have
one side pinned up, but it should have.

As he reached us, he took the puppy and received
a greeting as enthusiastic as the one Joe had gotten.
"Monte," he said, "you're a naughty fellow." He
looped the puppy's leash over his wrist firmly and
put the dog down on the grass. "Sit," he said. Monte
sat. Then his owner turned to us, giving a broad,
toothy grin. "Thanks for catching him."

"Actually, he caught us," I said. "He's a friendly
little guy. Did you call him Monte?"

The man smiled. "Yes. It's short for Montezuma. He's a chocolate Labrador."

"Ah," I said. "The Aztec emperor and fabled consumer of chocolate." I turned to Joe. "According to legend, Montezuma drank chocolate before visiting his harem."

"You're absolutely correct." The gray-haired man swept off his hat, giving me a look at a gorgeous head of hair. I also got a look at the even spacing around the hairline that showed that he'd had an expensive implant job.

"Maia Michaelson invited me to this—is it called the Rinkydink?" he said. "Have you seen her?"

"No." Joe and I both scanned the crowd. I bit my tongue before I could say *She's probably waiting to make an entrance.*

"I'm sure she'll be here in a minute," Joe said. "Is the wallet yours as well?"

I realized that I was still holding the oversized wallet with the big bills. I extended it to the gray-haired man just as a shrill voice called out. "Aubrey!"

"Here's Mae," I said. "I mean Maia." The two names were pronounced almost the same way, but they definitely referred to two different people.

Maia approached dramatically. Back when she was Mae Ensminger, this woman used to simply walk up. But the previous spring Mae had published a romantic novel under the nom de plume Maia Michaelson. According to the dictionary, I'd been told, the two names were pronounced the same way, but Mae called her new moniker "MAY-ah." In her new persona, Maia couldn't just walk up. She approached dramatically.

Becoming Maia Michaelson had changed Mae Ensminger drastically. Mae Ensminger was at least fifty. Maia Michaelson claimed to be only forty. Mae used to wear jeans and T-shirts, like the rest of us. Maia affected solid black from top-to-toe and wore big, clunky jewelry. Mae used to wear her mousy brown hair pulled into a ponytail, not unlike mine. Maia had coal black hair that hung down her back and was heavily teased on top of her head. Mae never wore makeup. But Maia wore lots of it. Mae used to stand with her back against the wall, observing, but not saying a lot. Maia talked all the time, in a voice that varied between too soft to understand and too piercing to bear. Maia theatrically gestured all the time. She hadn't gone as far as placing the back of her hand against her forehead and sighing, "Ah, me," but I wasn't going to be surprised when she did.

Maia—it definitely wasn't Mae—linked her arm through the gray-haired man's arm. "I see you've met Lee and Joe, Warner Pier's most glam young couple," she said.

"I don't know that we're particularly grim," I said. "I mean, glam! We're not very glamorous, and maybe not too young, but I'm Lee McKinney, and this is Joe Woodyard."

The gray-haired man shook hands with each of us. He'd hidden the wallet away someplace before I'd had a chance to ask him where he got the big bills.

He spoke. "I'm Aubrey Andrews Armstrong."

Sure you are, I thought. That name was as bogus as Maia Michaelson's. I spoke quickly to hide my thoughts—too quickly, I guess, because I pulled one of the malapropisms that make me sound like an idiot. "What brings you to Warner Pier, Mr. Strongarm? I mean, Mr. Armstrong!"

He blinked. Then he patted the hand Maia had placed on his arm and started to answer. But Maia spoke before he could. "No, Aubrey! You're not to tell a soul why you're here."

A frown flitted over Armstrong's face. "But, Maia, I know we haven't signed . . ."

"You can tell in a minute. But there's another person I want to hear the news first. That's why I insisted we come to the picnic. Lee, have you seen Maggie?"

Maggie McNutt? That was a surprise. Maia was about the only person in Warner Pier who didn't like Maggie.

"She's helping behind the serving table," Joe said. "I guess we'd better get in line, Lee."

We did so, followed by Maia and her new pal Aubrey. And behind them, I finally noticed, was Maia's husband—actually Mae's husband—Vernon Ensminger. "St. Vernon the Patient," Joe called him. Vernon was a big, bald guy—no implants on Vernon's scalp—who operated a successful fruit farm. His workboots and plaid shirt were so authentic that they made Aubrey Andrews Armstrong look more bogus than ever.

Joe stopped to speak to Vernon, which is typical of Joe. People tended to ignore Vernon, now that he was merely an adjunct to the colorful Maia Michaelson, but Joe had always liked him. I liked him, too. If you had a flat on a lonely road, Vernon Ensminger was the kind of guy who would drop by with a jack.

Maia, Aubrey, and Vernon stepped into line behind us. The puppy frisked up to me again, jumping on the back of my slacks this time. I was beginning to wonder if Aubrey Andrews Armstrong would be good for the dry cleaning bill.

Maia was craning her neck around, talking shrilly. "I do want you to meet Maggie. She's simply delightful. And so talented. This whole event was her idea. Oh, there's her husband. Ken! Ken!"

Ken McNutt had been heading for the parking lot, but he could hardly ignore her summons. He came over, looking as thin as usual. Thin was the word for Ken—thin build, thin hair, thin voice. Like Vernon, he stayed in the background and let his wife star.

Ken nodded to Vernon, then spoke. "Hello, Mae."

Maia didn't introduce Aubrey. "Where is your charming wife?"

"If you stay in line, you'll see her. She's in charge." He moved toward the parking lot again. "Sorry to run, but I have to be back for fifth period."

"Such a lovely young couple," Maia said, dripping condescension. "What my father called 'a teaching couple.'"

Joe seized the opportunity to speak quietly to me. "Why does Mae have it in for Maggie?"

I lowered my voice, too. "They both entered the Historical Society's competition for a dramatic sketch on the founding of Warner Pier. Maggie won."

Joe snorted. "That's something Maia will never forgive."

I shrugged. "Maggie avoids her. But this time she won't be able to."

Maggie had just come into view. She was standing beside the charcoal cooker where Mike Herrera, our mayor and one of Warner Pier's leading restaurateurs, was grilling bratwurst. Maia gave her a tremendous greeting, shrieking out her name.

I had to hand it to Maggie; she didn't visibly wince. She merely waved and picked up a Styrofoam plate, which she held close to Mike's elbow. He began to lift browned bratwurst from the grill to the plate. Maia had to wait until the serving line reached them before she could say anything else. But then she said plenty.

"Maggie! Maggie! Something wonderful has happened, and I want you to be the first to know."

As I say, Maggie was usually peppy as all get-out, but she didn't try to compete with Maia in the energy department. She spoke very quietly. "What is it, Maia?"

"This wonderful man is a Hollywood producer,

Maggie! He's buying the film rights to my book! And he wants to shoot the movie right here in Warner Pier!"

Maggie whipped her head in Maia's direction. Her mouth dropped slightly open, and her eyes grew large. Joe looked amazed, too, and I'm sure my jaw was hanging clear down to my chest. We all thought Maia's novel was awful. And someone wanted to make a movie of it?

Maia gave a triumphant crow. "Yes! A Hollywood producer, Maggie! This is Aubrey Andrews Armstrong!"

Maggie's eyes shifted to Aubrey Andrews Armstrong and grew even wider. She gave a startled gasp. She moved her right hand from under the Styrofoam plate. The plate broke in half and a dozen bratwurst landed in the grass of the Dock Street Park.

Chapter 2

We humans gasped, but Monte knew what to do. He nabbed one of those brats quicker than a flash of lightning out over Lake Michigan.

"Drop it, Monte!" Aubrey Andrews Armstrong sounded frantic. "It'll make him sick!"

It would take Superman to get a bratwurst away from a puppy as big as Monte, but Aubrey managed to get part of it. Joe and I used paper napkins to pick up the brats that had bounced under the serving table and out on our side, and Maggie picked up the ones that had fallen on her side. Mike Herrera muttered some Spanish word I pretended not to understand and reached for uncooked brats. "More brats in a minute, folks," he said. "If you want chicken, you're all set."

Joe and I decided we'd settle for chicken, though I normally prefer brats, and we moved on down the line. Behind me I could hear Maggie speaking graciously. "I'm delighted for you, Maia. A movie sale is quite a feather in your cap."

Maia introduced Aubrey Andrews Armstrong to Maggie. They exchanged how-do-you-dos.

"Well, well," Aubrey said. "Warner Pier certainly has a pretty little drama teacher. I'll bet the boys fight to get in your classes, Mrs. McNutt. Did I get your name right?"

"McNutt is correct, Mr. Armstrong."

Was it my imagination, or did Aubrey's few words sound not only sexist, but like a taunt? And had Maggie's reply sounded the same way?

Joe and I collected the rest of our lunch—rolls, slaw, potato salad, beans—and went to a picnic table. I found some hand cleaner in my purse, squirted some out, then passed the bottle to Joe. The memory of that dog slobber was fresh.

I was surprised when Armstrong came over. Maia wasn't with him. "May I join you?" he said. "Maia is table-hopping." He tied Monte's leash to the table leg, and told the pup to stay. Monte lay down.

"Monte seems well-trained for such a young dog," I said. "How old is he?"

"Four months. The key is to work with him twice a day, every day."

"I see you're an experienced dog owner."

Armstrong laughed. "You know what they say about Washington, D.C.? 'If you want a friend, get a dog.' That goes double for Hollywood, and I've been around the business all my life. I've always had a dog."

Joe spoke then. "I'm sorry, Mr. Armstrong, but I didn't catch the name of your production company."

"I don't think I threw it. It's Montezuma Movie Productions."

"Then I was wrong," I said. "Monte is named after your company, not after the Aztec emperor."

"No, you were right. Monte's name was inspired by the Aztec connection to chocolate, because he's a chocolate lab. I've always owned a chocolate lab. The company name had the same inspiration."

Joe ignored the chocolate lore. "What films has your company produced, Mr. Armstrong?"

"Call me Aubrey. We're indies, of course. Our current release is *Mimosa Magic*. And *Appaloosa* was a finalist at Sundance."

Joe nodded. "I haven't seen either of those, but I remember the reviews for *Mimosa Magic*. How long have you been a producer?"

Aubrey waved his hand. "Now you're asking a personal question—my age. What's your profession, Joe?"

"I'm Warner Pier city attorney."

Joe's answer surprised me. It was true, of course. But Joe's job advising the city council took him only a few hours a week, and it paid proportionally. His full-time job was restoring antique power boats—a business that was finally looking up financially. He usually identified himself as a boat repairman, ignoring his law degree unless he was doing city business.

Aubrey's eyes widened, just slightly, but if he was surprised to be having lunch with the city attorney, it didn't affect his tongue. He kept right on prattling away about the movies he'd made and the locations he'd used. He dropped names even I had heard—Robert R., Tom H., the C. brothers—and he talked about "the business."

After twenty minutes I'd decided Aubrey was as phony as his hairdo. I didn't make the rounds of the Texas beauty pageant circuit—I mean, scholarship pageant circuit—without learning a few things. When you meet the promoters who are around trying to take advantage of the naivete of the inexperienced girls in those competitions—well, there's a reason contestants are required to have older women as escorts. And I still fell for one of the jerks, the guy who was now my ex-husband.

Of course, putting up a phony front didn't mean Aubrey wasn't a legitimate movie producer any more than it meant all the guys lurking at the Miss Texas

Pageant were crooks. It just meant they might be.
And it meant they weren't the kind of people I
wanted to seek out as friends.

So I was annoyed when Joe announced he needed
to talk to the mayor, then got up and disappeared,
leaving me stuck with Aubrey and the dog. But his
disappearance gave me a chance to ask a question.
"Are you a coin collector, Mr. Armstrong?"

He smiled broadly. "Why, no. Do I look like one?"

"I expect they come in all sizes and shapes. I just
wondered about the big bills Monte brought me."

I'll swear that Aubrey Andrews Armstrong
blushed. If he didn't actually turn red, he squirmed
like a little kid, and he laughed weakly before he
answered me. "Oh, those were just props," he said.
"I really can't say more."

He launched into another tale about the C. brothers, but I was hardly listening. My question might
have been a bit nosy, but it was logical. Since I'd
seen the big bills, and Aubrey knew I'd seen them,
I was bound to wonder.

I shrugged mentally and looked around for Maia.
I'd had enough of her tame movie producer, and I
was hoping she'd rescue me. She wasn't in view, but
I did see Aunt Nettie.

My dear aunt and employer, Jeannette TenHuis,
has beautiful white hair, bright blue eyes, and that
solid look I associate with a lifetime spent eating sub-
stantial Dutch cooking. She was wearing her usual
workday garb—a white food-service uniform—
topped by a blue sweater, and was carrying bratwurst and potato salad on a Styrofoam plate. I
waved. She smiled her sunny smile and came over.
"May I join you?"

Aubrey jumped to his feet—not an easy trick when
you're sitting at a picnic table—and swept off his
outback hat as I introduced them.

"Aubrey's thinking of producing a movie of Maia's novel," I said. "He might film here in Warner Pier."

"How exciting!" Aunt Nettie said. "That would be a real thrill. This is a small town. We don't get a lot of glamour."

Her answer surprised me, since only a few years earlier one of the year's biggest Hollywood productions, starring Tom H., had used locations within ten miles of Warner Pier. Aubrey Andrews Armstrong was not the first producer to discover the beauty of the Lake Michigan beaches, the charm of our lush farmland, and the quaintness of our villages.

"Oh, filmmaking isn't all glamour," Aubrey said. "Your niece says she works in the shop which made those fabulous chocolates I see over there on the dessert table. Now that's glamour! Are you connected with chocolate, too?"

Aunt Nettie dropped her eyes modestly, and I answered his question. "Aunt Nettie is the owner of TenHuis Chocolade."

"We ship European-style bonbons, truffles, and molded chocolates nationwide," Aunt Nettie said. "Lee is our business manager. She keeps our finances in excellent order."

It was as if a light went on behind Aubrey Andrews Armstrong's eyes. He turned the full force of his personality on Aunt Nettie. First, he insisted on trying some TenHuis chocolates. ("I'll be right back. Monte, stay!") Then he gushed over their quality. ("Do you do gift packages? This is exactly what I need to send Meg for her birthday next week. Few people know that she's a slave to chocolate. I don't know how she keeps that great figure.") Then he did his Hollywood producer act for Aunt Nettie, referring once again to Tom H. and Robert R. and Michael D.

The weirdest part to me was that Aunt Nettie ate

it up, scarfing up his act along with her bratwurst and potato salad. She even cooed at the dog, scratching him under the chin. "You're as beautiful as the molded pups we have over at the shop," she said. "But I know you can't eat one."

Aubrey beamed. "Good for you. It's amazing how many people don't know chocolate can be poisonous to dogs."

I'll swear Aunt Nettie simpered. "I don't know much about dogs, but I know a lot about chocolate."

I was ready to prick Aubrey Andrews Armstrong with a pin to see if the hot air would rush out by the time Maia finally showed up. But that didn't really help the situation. A second person showed up at the same time: six feet, three inches of redhead with the poetic name of Dolly Jolly.

"Can I join you?" she yelled.

Everything about Dolly is big: her build, which is something like a pro-football lineman; her voice, which could shatter a plate glass window; her hair, which is a vivid natural red; her personality, which is unforgettable. When she sat down at the picnic table I felt as if we'd been struck by a volcanic eruption.

I'd first met Dolly early in the summer, when she'd rented a remote cottage near Warner Pier while she finished writing a cookbook. In September, Dolly had rented the apartment over TenHuis Chocolade, and two weeks earlier she had begun working for Aunt Nettie, learning the craft of making fine chocolates.

To my surprise Dolly wasn't carrying a plate of bratwurst or of chicken. Apparently she wasn't looking for lunch companions. I wondered why she'd joined us.

We introduced her to Aubrey Andrews Armstrong, but she merely nodded to him. To my surprise she turned her full attention—which is like being pinned down by a searchlight—to Maia. Apparently Dolly had come to our table because she wanted to know all about Maia's novel. But because Maia wanted to talk to Aubrey, she didn't want to discuss her novel. This made the resulting conversation pretty nonsensical.

"Loved your book!" Dolly shouted. As I said, Dolly always talks at top decibels. "How much is based on fact?"

"Oh, it all is," Maia said. "Of course, it's been sifted through the artistic process." She turned to Aubrey. "I'm sorry I left you so long. Vernon had to catch up with his deer-hunting buddies. Then I ran into Chuck O'Riley, the editor of our little newspaper. He'll be over to interview you in a few minutes."

"Fine, fine," Armstrong said. "I was just talking to Mrs. TenHuis."

Before Maia could acknowledge Aunt Nettie's presence, Dolly jumped in again. "Julia's old father! Interesting character! Really crusty! Is he based on the real man?"

She was too loud for Maia to ignore. "Yes, he is. He was my grandfather, you know. I remember how he terrified me as a child." She turned back to Aubrey. "Nettie's one of our leading entrepreneurs."

Aunt Nettie shook her head. "Entrepreneur is too grand a word for a cook."

Dolly was not to be denied. She was still concentrating on Maia. "The stepmother! Between a rock and a hard place! Felt sorry for her!"

Maia looked surprised as she pulled her attention away from the movie producer and answered Dolly. "It's interesting that you should see that. From Julia's viewpoint, she was a genuine 'wicked stepmother.' But she was my grandmother. Of course, she died young, so I didn't know her."

"She was young! She might have been attracted to Dennis Grundy herself!"

This was apparently a new idea to Maia. She looked a little shocked, but she didn't reply. Instead she looked around the park. "Where's Chuck, I wonder?"

"In Hollywood," Aubrey said. Or I thought he did. Then I realized that he was answering some question Aunt Nettie had asked. At least three conversations were bouncing around that table, and I'd completely lost track of who was talking about what. I was relieved when Tracy Roderick came over and spoke to me softly.

"Mrs. McNutt wants to talk to you," she said.

I was delighted to leave. I went around behind the serving line and called to Maggie.

She came over immediately, and she grasped my arm. "Did Joe leave?"

"He disappeared, but as far as I know he's still here, Maggie. What's wrong?"

"Oh, I can't find Chief Jones. I can't find Joe. I don't know who else I could talk to."

This dithering was most unlike the efficient and focused Maggie. "Why do you need them?"

She made a gesture that was awfully close to wringing her hands. "I don't know. Maybe I don't need them. It's just—Oh, god! Here he comes."

I looked around to see Aubrey Andrews Armstrong approaching.

Maggie spoke loudly. "I appreciate that, Lee. And I'd appreciate it if you'll tell Nettie the chocolates are the hit of the picnic. I'll be by later to thank her personally."

Aubrey and Monte arrived. Aubrey was grinning broadly. "Mrs. McNutt"—he still was making that name sound really odd—"Mrs. McNutt, I think you had a brilliant idea."

"What was that, Mr. Armstrong?" Maggie sounded funny, too.

I moved away as Aubrey spoke again. "This Rinkydink! Such a clever project. . . ."

Their voices faded, and I went back to my picnic table to join Aunt Nettie. I didn't understand why Maggie was upset. Why did she want to talk to the police chief? Why did she not want to talk to Aubrey Andrews Armstrong? She could have spotted him as a phony, of course. But I had, too, and I wasn't incoherent over it. Besides, even if Armstrong was a phony, it was no skin off my nose. If he was up to no good, his target was apparently Maia, not me. Maia had Vernon to watch over her, and Vernon was really good at guarding Maia. I wasn't really worried about Maia. Maggie and Maia weren't exactly friends. Why would Maggie care if some Hollywood-type made Maia look silly?

When I got back to the table, Dolly had gone. Aunt Nettie was alone with Maia. Maia was tossing her artificially black hair and giggling, while Aunt Nettie sat smiling her usual sweet smile.

"Oh, Lee," Maia said. "Guess what!"

"I can't imagine."

"Tell her, Nettie!"

"It's nice, Maia, but I don't want to make too much of it."

I was getting annoyed with Maia. "Make too much of what?"

Maia widened her eyes. "Nettie's got a date," she said. "With Aubrey."

I hope I didn't gasp in amazement. Or dismay. After all, Aunt Nettie had been a widow for more than two years. If she wanted to go out on a date, I really ought to encourage her. I ought to be thrilled for her. And I would have been, if she'd been invited out by anybody but Aubrey Andrews Armstrong.

Because Aubrey might seem like a phony to me, but he was attractive. I didn't doubt that he could, if he wished, cut quite a swath among the single women of Warner Pier. So why had he selected Aunt Nettie? She was full of wisdom and character and loving-kindness, true. These wonderful qualities, frankly, are not known for attracting middle-aged men vain enough to get hair implants. No, those guys are usually hoping the hair implants will attract younger women.

Had Maia promoted this date? If so, why? I'd been under the impression that Maia was thinking of Aubrey as her own catch—perhaps not romantically, with Vernon always guarding her. But I'd have expected her to be somewhat jealous if Aubrey paid attention to someone besides her.

I was stunned. But I had to say something. So I did.

"That's wonderland!" I said. "I mean, that's wonderful!"

Aunt Nettie, who knows about my twisted tongue, shot me an amused glance. Darn her. She always sees right through me.

I didn't have a chance to say anything more. Maia was talking again. "It was all Aubrey's idea," she said. "He invited Vernon and me to go out to dinner at the Warner River Lodge tonight, and he just turned to Nettie and asked her to join the party."

Aunt Nettie was still smiling. "It's not exactly a date. Aubrey simply wanted a companion."

"Don't sell yourself short, Nettie! I can tell that he's quite taken with you." Maia's voice was growing shrill. I decided she might be jealous after all.

"Any intelligent person would be taken with Aunt Nettie," I said. "And the Warner River Lodge is a marvelous place for dinner. It ought to be a nice evening."

Aunt Nettie stood up and collected the debris of her lunch. "I'm looking forward to it," she said. "I guess I'd better get back to the shop."

"We'd both better do that," I said. I gathered my own debris—plus Joe's, since he'd never showed up again—said good-bye to Maia, and followed Aunt Nettie to the trash can. That's when I saw Joe. He was over on the other side of the picnic shelter, talking to Mayor Mike Herrera and Warner Pier's police chief, Hogan Jones.

"I'll just tell Joe I'm leaving," I said.

Aunt Nettie headed toward the shop, and I veered off and walked over to Joe, Mike and Hogan Jones. Mike, and Joe looked solemn, but Chief Jones—a tall skinny guy who could easily find work as an Abraham Lincoln impersonator—formed his craggy face into a big grin as I walked up. "Hi, Lee. What do you think of our Hollywood producer?"

"He's definitely Mr. Personality."

"Ain't he, though. Did he tell you that you oughta be in pictures?"

"No, he saved his charm for Aunt Nettie. He's taking her out to dinner."

Joe whistled, and Mike said that Spanish word I pretend not to understand.

"They're going to the Warner River Lodge with Maia and Vernon," I said. "I first thought it was Maia's idea, but apparently Aubrey came up with the invitation without prompting."

The chief grinned even more broadly. "And you don't like it."

I looked around to make sure Aubrey or Maia or Aunt Nettie hadn't crept up behind me. "I guess I ought to be glad if Aunt Nettie developed a real social life," I said. "She's been much too close to the business since Uncle Phil died. And I think I would be happy for her if . . . well, if we knew a little more about this guy. I'm afraid he's the type who sees himself as a heartbreaker, and she's not exactly up on the current dating scene."

Joe jumped in with, "Don't wo—" but Chief Jones cut him off sharply.

"Now, listen, Lee," he said. "Nettie's a grown woman, and if she wants to have a little fling, you just stay out of it."

I could have kicked him. I'm sure I pursed my lips until they disappeared before I spoke. "Chief Jones . . . Hogan . . . there's nothing I would like better than to see Aunt Nettie get some fun out of life."

"You sure don't act like it. You youngsters think all us old folks are so far over the hill that we can't remember passing the top."

"Aunt Nettie's not over the hill! She's sharper than I am at nearly everything. But this Armstrong—his eyes lit up like he'd hit the jackpot when she said she owned her own business."

Unfortunately for Joe, he decided to join the argument. "Lee, the chief just means—"

"I know what he means! He means I'm aghast. I mean, ageist! Well, I'm not! Aunt Nettie's got tons more brains than I have, but she's never had to deal with a guy like Aubrey Andrews Armstrong."

Before I could go on, a voice boomed out right behind me. "Just stay away from my place! I don't consider leaving a business card under an apple as asking permission to trespass on a man's property."

"But Uncle Silas, he wanted to see the historic site—"

"I don't care if he wanted to see the Statue of Liberty! I don't want to catch another one of those gol-durned treasure hunters in my orchard. The next one is likely to get a load of pea shot in his hind end—and I don't care if he's a local kid or some big Hollywood producer!"

Chapter 3

There was an argument going on behind me, and it was louder than the one I was having with Chief Jones about Aunt Nettie's romantic life.

I heard the second voice again, and this time I recognized it.

"You old silly!" The arch tones could only belong to Maia Michaelson. When I turned around I saw that she was facing an old man who was wearing work clothes even more authentic than Vernon's. Maia laughed merrily and went on. "Don't you know you could make money if they use your property?"

"Make money the way you have? By raking up a scandal? I'd be ashamed."

"What do you mean?"

"Writing about that old story. It doesn't do any credit to the family. Or to you!"

"Why, Uncle Silas! You simply don't have a romantic soul."

"Romantic, my foot! Disreputable! Scandalous!"

Maia smiled, but her smile looked angry. She leaned close to the old man. They were much the same height, the top of her teased hair was even with the dirty baseball cap he wore. "Now, Uncle Silas—"

But the old man wasn't having any. "I don't want to hear any more about this foolishness," he said. He wasn't quite yelling. "It's not women's business! It's sure not the business of stupid women who shame the family!"

Vernon suddenly appeared between the two combatants. "Come on, Mae," he said. "You can talk to your uncle later."

But Silas turned on him. "And I blame you, Vernon. Encouraging her in this silliness! She ought to be in the kitchen canning, not making a fool of herself with this writing nonsense. You should have stopped her."

Vernon drew himself up, and I realized what a big man he was. "I'm proud of Mae," he said. "And you should be, too."

Then he turned away, guiding Maia-Mae in front of him, escorting her for all the world like a bodyguard with a princess.

The old man snorted angrily and walked away in a different direction, crossing Dock Street and walking toward a beat-up old pickup.

I checked to make sure that Maia and Vernon were out of earshot; then I turned to the three city officials I'd been talking to, Joe, Chief Hogan Jones, and Mayor Mike Herrera. "Who's the literary critic?"

Joe laughed, Mike rolled his eyes, and Hogan Jones spoke. "Silas Snow," he said. "He's an uncle to Mae or Maia or whoever she is these days."

"I gather he's not excited about the prospect of a movie of her book being filmed."

Joe answered me. "I guess he's also not excited about having the movie shot on his property. It's the farm at the Haven Road exit. The one with the fruit stand."

"The stand that's all pumpkins right at the moment?"

"Yeah. Not that every fruit stand in the Midwest isn't covered with pumpkins this time of the year.

But it's the farm where the real-life story of Maia's book supposedly happened."

"Do you mean that Julia Snow and Dennis Grundy actually existed?"

This time all three of them shrugged. Chief Jones spoke. "You'd have to look up the records to see if there's any truth to her tale. I doubt it happened exactly that way." He walked away, followed by Mike Herrera.

I spoke to Joe. "I knew Maia's book was based on some sort of local legend, but I didn't know it was a family story."

"Every town up and down Lake Michigan has some old tale about Chicago gangsters, you know."

"If all those stories were true, there would have been more gangsters than peach growers around the lake."

"True. But supposedly Al Capone did have a camp of some sort on the Upper Peninsula."

"That's hundreds of miles from here."

Joe nodded. "But back in the twenties and thirties, lots of farmers had little cottages they rented to tourists, just the way a few of them still do. Some of them had docks where cargo could be shifted quietly. And sometimes questionable people rented those cottages."

"Just the way they could now."

"Yeah. Anyway, from what I heard at my grandmother's knee, I'm guessing that Silas Snow's father, Mae Ensminger's grandfather, had a cottage like that back in the woods, with a path down to a creek where it was possible to land a small boat. Apparently old Mr. Snow rented it without asking for references. The story is that a young tough guy from Chicago rented it for a whole summer sometime in the late twenties. Everybody local assumed he was hiding out from the law."

"And the Snows had a daughter."

"Right. An older half sister to Silas and to Mae's mom. That's part of the story. Don't ask me if it was a big romance or something sleazy or nothing at all. I guess there was talk at the time."

"Seventy-five years ago, and it's still an item."

"You knew this was a small town when you moved here, Lee. Part of the story, naturally, is buried treasure. The bank loot—or whatever—is supposed to be hidden someplace on the old farm."

"Now owned by Silas Snow?"

"Right. Going out there and digging around is a Warner Pier High School tradition. Heck, I did it!"

"It's apparently a tradition that annoys Silas Snow. But what became of the supposed gangster? And what became of the farmer's daughter?"

"I don't know. Julia Snow and Dennis Grundy both left Warner Pier, but I don't know if they went separately or together. The Snow family never mentioned Julia after that. Maia thinks the two of them lived happily ever after."

"And Uncle Silas doesn't. And I'm not interested enough to research the matter. I've got to get back to the office."

As I started to go, I saw Aubrey, who now was the center of a group of drama club members. Maggie was not in sight, but seeing Aubrey reminded me of her.

I turned back to Joe. "Did Maggie talk to you?"

"We said hi when you and I went through the line."

"No, this was after that. She acted sort of frantic."

"I'll check with her. And I'll see you later."

As I walked toward the office my mind bounced back to Aunt Nettie and her date with Aubrey Andrews Armstrong. Even more surprising than the date was Hogan Jones's reaction to it. Hogan might be a small-town police chief now, but he'd spent years in law enforcement in a major city. He ought to be wary of people who drop in unannounced and claim to be movie producers. But he thought it was fine for Aunt Nettie to go out with this stranger. He'd accused me of treating my aunt as if she were senile. Or at least too old to have any interest in romance.

Nobody ever gets that old, do they? I knew Aunt Nettie and her friends were still interested. They had coffee klatches in our break room now and then, and snickered over various older gents in Warner Pier. This one was considered too decrepit, that one too much of a dirty old man, another too hung up on his deceased wife.

Oddly enough, the only one they all seemed to approve of was—ta-dah!—Hogan Jones. But Hogan had so far deftly avoided all the invitations of Warner Pier's widows. And if he had himself ever asked anyone out, I hadn't heard about it.

I was trying to refocus my thoughts on TenHuis Chocolade's accounts receivable when Joe caught up with me.

"I'll walk back with you," he said. "My truck's over that way."

"What did Maggie want?"

"Nothing. She said she had solved her problem, and she didn't tell me what it was."

"Good for her. Now I can concentrate on worrying about Aunt Nettie."

"I wish you wouldn't. Like the chief says—"

"Joe, don't start telling me she's a grown woman. I know that. But she's been a big help to me, and I'd be negligent if I stood by and let her get hurt."

"But Nettie's not your responsibility, Lee."

"Of course she's my responsibility! Who else does she have?"

Joe stopped abruptly. "She has herself! You don't have to take care of her! Maybe that's our problem."

"Our problem? Ours! What problem do we have?"

"Getting married. I want to get married, Lee. And I can't get you to set a date. I can't even get you to say that you'll set one eventually."

I closed my eyes and sighed. "How did we get from Aunt Nettie to this?"

"I think you're hiding behind her. You can't even consider getting married and leaving darling Aunt Nettie alone."

"I've never said that! I never even thought that!"

"It's the only explanation I can come up with. You claim you love me, but I can't pin you down."

"Joe, you have lost your mind. I'll plead guilty to the charge of being wishy-washy about getting married, but it has nothing to do with Aunt Nettie. And I'm not going to argue about this in the middle of Peach Street. Good-bye."

I walked away, and Joe stood where he'd been. I didn't look back. I was too mad, and maybe too scared. Because Joe had come up with a new wrinkle in an argument that had been going on since the previous June, when Joe had first told me he wanted to marry me.

Or had he? Frankly, whenever he brought it up, he used the phrase he'd just declaimed. "I want to get married." Somehow that wasn't the same as saying, "I want to marry you."

But this was the first time Aunt Nettie had figured in the argument.

I was ready to admit that Aunt Nettie was special to me. Twice in my life—first when I was sixteen and my parents were getting a divorce and later when my own marriage broke up—she'd stepped in, given me a home, and made me feel that I was a worthwhile person even if my life was in shambles. If I had a shred of mental health, I owed it to Aunt Nettie. And she wasn't even a blood relation; she was my mother's brother's widow.

But the last thing Aunt Nettie would want was to come between Joe and me. She had made it clear that she approved of Joe.

Right at that moment I wasn't sure I did. I walked on, mulling over how quickly my life had changed from happy to horrendous. An hour earlier I'd been enjoying the lovely fall day with nothing on my mind but delivering chocolates to the Rinkydink. Now I was frantically worried about a charmer who was broadcasting phony signals and moving in on my aunt, and I'd had an argument with my boyfriend.

I needed comfort. I resolved not to think about my problems for the rest of the afternoon. I couldn't settle the question of whether or not I wanted to marry Joe while I was upset, and I couldn't risk quarreling with Aunt Nettie by making any overt attack on Aubrey Andrews Armstrong.

As I went in the door to TenHuis Chocolade ("Handmade chocolates in the Dutch tradition"), I breathed deeply to get the full effect of the chocolate aroma. After I've been inside for a little while, I get used to it, so whenever I come in I try to inhale all the chocolate atmosphere I can.

TenHuis Chocolade is my real home, I guess. For one thing, Aunt Nettie and I spend more time there than we do in her hundred-year-old house on Lake Shore Drive, the place where we sleep and store our clothes. For another, it's a friendly place—a cozy retail shop, a shiny-clean workroom, and a comfortable break room.

As I came in I could see Aunt Nettie through the big glass windows that separate our small retail shop from the big workroom where the chocolates are made. She was standing beside Dolly Jolly. I could tell by the color of the substance on the worktable that Aunt Nettie was teaching Dolly to roll uniform balls of strawberry-flavored filling for strawberry truffles. ("White chocolate and strawberry interior coated in dark chocolate.") Dolly was sticking out the tip of her tongue, a sign that she was concentrating.

I couldn't hear what Aunt Nettie was saying, but I could see Dolly roll a ball of pink soft filling, compare it to one Aunt Nettie had formed, then set it on a scale. After more than thirty years in the chocolate business, Aunt Nettie can roll those balls for hours on end and have every one come out within a microgram of every other one. This is a trick that the "hairnet ladies," the skilled workers who actually produce TenHuis Chocolade, claim a chimpanzee can do. And maybe a chimpanzee could—once she'd had enough practice. But you have to learn to judge exactly how big to make the little balls. The truffle fillings have to be uniform; we can't sell Customer A one that's larger than the one we sell Customer B.

Dolly Jolly was looming over Aunt Nettie just the way she looms over everybody.

"I think I'm getting the hang of it!" Dolly shouted.

"Those look good," Aunt Nettie said. "It only takes a couple of rolls to get them round. You don't have to handle them a lot. Now you can start rolling them in chocolate."

Dolly took a metal bowl over to the vat of dark chocolate. She used the spigot at the bottom of the vat to drain chocolate into the bowl, then turned to Aunt Nettie, looking quizzical.

"A little more chocolate will make it easier to work with," Aunt Nettie said.

I walked over to them. "Where'd you disappear to, Dolly? I got up to talk to Maggie McNutt, and when I came back you were gone."

Dolly's face turned even redder than it usually is. "I had to get back to work," she said. For once her voice didn't boom. In fact, I could hardly hear her. "Just wanted to meet Maia Michaelson."

"What did you think of her?"

Dolly shrugged. "Glad I'm not part of her family," she said.

"Yeah, being related to Maia is a scary thought," I said.

Dolly didn't seem inclined to make any further comment, so I left Aunt Nettie showing Dolly how to roll truffles and went into my office. My office is a glass cubicle between the shop and the workroom. It's not as homey as the rest of TenHuis Chocolade, I guess, but during the pre-Christmas rush I almost live there. I glanced at the framed picture of Joe standing beside his favorite antique wooden boat. I wasn't going to think about Joe that afternoon, so I laid it facedown.

The chocolate business is seasonal, and the seasons start with Halloween and end with Mother's Day. With October a third gone, we were past Halloween preparations, almost through with Thanksgiving, and well into Christmas. Dolly might be learning to roll truffles, but most of the other employees were molding Santa Claus figures and filling chocolate Christmas tree ornaments with tiny chocolate toys. Toward the back of the room, eight women were standing around a big stainless steel table, wrapping cubes of molded chocolate in gorgeous foils to produce chocolates that looked like tiny little gift boxes.

The scene was giving me the dose of comfort that I needed. I sat at my desk and counted my blessings for a minute. When I'd left Dallas a year and a half earlier, I'd been recovering from a lousy marriage and a mean-spirited divorce. I had finally finished my degree in accounting, but it had been a struggle. TenHuis Chocolade hadn't been in very good shape, either. My uncle Phil had always handled the business side. When he was killed by a drunk driver, the whole thing had been dumped on Aunt Nettie, who made wonderful chocolates, but hated to balance her checkbook. After I'd taken over as business manager, I'd discovered unpaid bills, lousy customer relations, and poor shipping schedules.

Now Aunt Nettie's unconditional love had given me a new sense of my own worth. I'd formed a circle of friends I felt I could rely on—even if my boyfriend was acting like a jerk right at the moment. TenHuis was back on a firm financial foundation, with chocolates shipped on time and all the bills paid. I could honestly say I'd accomplished a lot.

Then I caught sight of our fall display of molded chocolates on the shelf behind the cash register. Aunt Nettie called it "Pet Parade." It featured tiny figures of puppies and kittens in dark, white, and milk chocolate. Some of them were even spotted dogs with lop ears, dark chocolate with white spots, or white chocolate with milk chocolate spots. There were tiny baskets of kittens or puppies. Each little animal was darling. My Texas grandma would have said each one was cuter than a spotted pup under a red wagon. In fact, a five-inch toy red wagon filled with one-inch puppies had been one of our best sellers that fall.

But now those puppies made Monte and his owner flash into my mind.

What if Aunt Nettie really fell for Aubrey Andrews Armstrong? She could get badly hurt. I couldn't stand that idea.

But, as Chief Jones had pointed out, Aunt Nettie was a grown woman. He was right. I had no right to influence her. I'd have to be gracious about Aubrey.

I smiled brightly into my computer screen. "Have a nice evening," I said sweetly.

I might see Aubrey as a real threat, but I had to keep my mouth shut about it.

I stuck to that resolve for an hour. Until Maggie McNutt came into the shop.

CHOCOLATE CHAT

IT'S ALL (NOT) RELATIVE

The tree that gives us chocolate was assigned the scientific name *Theobroma cacao* by the Swedish scientist Linnaeus in 1753. *Theobroma* can be translated as "food of the gods," a name that not only reflects the legends of the pre-Columbian Indians as to its origins but also seems to be a comment on its heavenly appeal to the sense of taste.

The dried and roasted seeds of the cacao tree are processed to form cocoa, which is how "cacao" is usually pronounced in American English. Despite the sound-alike, it has no relationship to the coconut palm, *Cocos nucifera,* though products of this plant are sometimes called "coco."

Neither is it related to the coca bush, *Erythroxylum coca.* This plant is used for a tea sometimes used to relieve symptoms of altitude sickness. But its greatest use is in producing cocaine.

So, let's get this straight. Chocolate and cocaine are not produced from the same plant. The high chocoholics get from indulging in truffles, bonbons, or plain old solid chocolate is not an illicit form of bliss, and chocolate is not physically addictive. Saying that chocolate is not habit-forming, however, might be going too far.

Chapter 4

Despite my resolve, I guess I had never stopped worrying about Aubrey. Anyway, shortly after three p.m. Maggie McNutt came in the front door of TenHuis Chocolade carrying two large trays, and as soon as I saw her, the movie producer popped into my mind.

I recognized the trays as the heavy foil ones we'd used to display our donated chocolates, and I went out to the shop to meet Maggie. "Those are just throwaway trays," I said. "You didn't have to return them."

Maggie spoke in a low voice. "I wanted an excuse to speak to you," she said. "I need a favor."

"Sure. As long as it has nothing to do with Aubrey Andrews Armstrong."

Maggie's eyes popped. If she'd been holding another plate of bratwurst, I feel sure she would have dropped it. "Why did you say that?" she said.

"I guess he made quite an impression on me."

"What kind of impression?"

"Oh, he reminded me of a lot of the promoters I

met back when I did the Miss Texas pageant. What kind of favor do you need?"

My answer seemed to calm Maggie. "Are you on speaking terms with Maia Michaelson?"

"I rarely have anything to say to her, but I guess we're on speaking terms."

"Well, I'm not. But she needs to be warned about this . . . this Armstrong."

"You make the name sound like a curse." I lowered my voice. "What do you know about him?"

"Not much! I mean, nothing! Nothing at all! I mean, I'm like you. He's the kind of promoter you spot around beauty pageants and talent shows. Some of them are legit. Some are not. They just need to be approached with caution, and Maia seems to be swallowing his act without question."

"Maia's not the only one. Aubrey has invited Aunt Nettie out to dinner."

"Gosh! Can you keep her from going?"

"How? She's a grown-up woman and a lot smarter than I am. If I say anything, it's going to make me look as if I don't want her to get out and have a social life."

Maggie put her elbows on the top of our showcase and dropped her head into her hands. She obviously wasn't looking at the chocolate puppy dogs inside. She seemed close to despair. "What am I going to do?" she said.

She'd barely finished asking herself that when the door to the shop swung open, and of all the people in Warner Pier, who should walk in but Mae Ensminger, also known as Maia Michaelson.

I'm sure I looked guilty. "Oh!" I said. "Hi, Mae! I mean, Maia!"

Maia tossed her black curls and laughed her merry laugh before she spoke. "Hello, Lee. Hello, Maggie. Is Nettie busy? I thought we ought to coordinate our wardrobes for tonight."

Coordinate their wardrobes? Like junior high? "I'll see if Aunt Nettie can come up front," I said. "She's training a new warning. I mean, worker! She's training a new employee."

I slunk back to the workroom. Why does my tongue insist on embarrassing me like that?

At least, I thought, Maggie and Maia weren't speaking, so it seemed safe to leave them alone together. But a minute later, when Aunt Nettie and I came back to the shop, they *were* speaking. And both of them sounded angry.

"More worthwhile than a stupid romance novel," Maggie said.

"Not romance! Mainstream!" Maia countered. "And now a screenplay!"

"Of all the gullible—" Maggie spit out the words, but in midsentence she stopped talking. Her face became pale. I realized she was looking at the door to the shop, and that it was opening.

Aubrey put his head inside and spoke. "Are you nearly ready, Maia? I'm sure that Ms. Nettie and her charming niece can't allow me to bring Monte inside."

Maia's voice fluted. "I'll be right out. Maggie McNutt was just leaving, going back to her sweet little high school students."

Maggie shot Maia a look that would have been lethal to a normal person. Then Aubrey stepped back and held the door open for Maggie. She marched past him without a word.

Maia laughed. "Now, Nettie . . ." she began. I went into my office and did something I rarely do. I closed the door. It was glass, like the walls, so I could still see Maia posturing and posing in the shop. But at least her voice wasn't as loud.

I stared at the computer again, and again practiced seeing Aunt Nettie off on her date. I gave a parody of a smile. "Have a nice evening," I said.

I was truly unhappy about Aunt Nettie being involved for even one evening with Aubrey Andrews Armstrong. But it was none of my affair. She would never interfere with my love life, and I had no right to interfere with hers. Butt out, Lee, I told myself firmly. And keep out of Maia's life, too. She's another grown woman. It's none of your business.

I kept my eyes on the computer screen until Maia left the shop, but when the bell on the door rang again I looked up. That afternoon we had no counter staff, so if anybody wanted to buy chocolates, it was my job to wait on them.

The person who came rushing in wasn't a customer. It was Tracy Roderick, our summer employee—Tracy of the stringy hair, who'd been elected president of the drama club and who had been staffing the dessert table at the Rinkydink.

Tracy rushed over to my office and opened the door. "Can I come in?"

"Sure, Tracy. What can I do for you?"

"My hair! I've got to do something about it."

I stared at her. Yes, Tracy needed a new hairstyle. I knew her mother had been trying to get her do something about it for a year. But now Tracy was acting as if it were an emergency.

"Why?" I said. "I mean, what brought on this decision?"

"I might have a chance at a part in a movie, Lee!"

"What?"

"You met that movie producer, Mr. Armstrong! I saw you talking to him. Isn't he divine?"

"He's certainly not an ordinary human, so maybe he is divine. What did he say?"

"He told us he's going to hire people in Warner Pier for small roles in the film he's going to shoot. The drama club's going to have a special meeting about it." Tracy clutched her hands together and held them to her chin in a semiprayerful attitude. "Oh, Lee! It could be my big chance! Will you help me?"

I stared at Tracy in utter dismay. I'd just convinced myself that Aunt Nettie and Maia were old enough to take care of themselves, that I should keep quiet about my misgivings about Aubrey Andrews Armstrong.

But now Aubrey had moved in on the high school drama students. They weren't grown-ups; they were young and inexperienced and would be easy for him to exploit. I couldn't stand by and let that happen, but I didn't have the heart to tell Tracy that. And she was waiting for an answer.

"Sure, Tracy," I said. "I'll help you with your makeup, and I'll make an appointment at Angie's for you. I'll go with you, if you like. Angie gives the best haircuts in Warner Pier, and if you need highlights or something, she'll advise you."

"Oh, thank you, Lee! That will be wonderful!" She bounced up and down. "I've got the money I saved last summer. I can take it out of my college fund. I'm just so excited!"

"Angie shouldn't be busy, now that the summer people are gone," I said. "I'll see if she can get you in tomorrow evening. I've got to do some research tonight."

Yes, I'd be busy that evening. I had to try to find out something about Aubrey Andrews Armstrong and Montezuma Motion Pictures. And I didn't want to tell anybody what I was doing. Especially not Joe. Not that there was any reason to expect I'd have the opportunity to tell Joe anything that night. I had the feeling he was as mad at me as I was at him.

So I played business manager until five o'clock, taking orders over the telephone, checking the Ten-Huis e-mail for more orders, and calling suppliers. In between I worked on the payroll. If business kept improving, I was going to need an assistant.

But closing time finally came. I told Aunt Nettie I was going to grab dinner downtown, then work late.

She seemed a bit disappointed that I wouldn't be home to see her off on her dinner date.

"I'll be home by the time Aubrey brings you in," I said. "In case you need a chaplain. I mean, a chaperone!"

Aunt Nettie laughed. "I don't anticipate needing either. But I'm almost sorry I said I'd go."

"It ought to be fun. Aubrey's a charmer."

"I'm looking forward to spending some time with him. And Vernon's a nice person. But Mae has gone crazy."

"You can put up with her for one evening."

Aunt Nettie left. I pulled the shades on the street door and on the show windows, then turned to my computer. That would be the easiest place to start my check of movie producers. I went on line, called up Google, and typed in "Aubrey Andrews Armstrong."

An hour later I'd found out something very interesting. Aubrey Andrews Armstrong apparently didn't exist. At least I couldn't find him under that name.

A general search for his highly distinctive name brought nothing. A prowl through the Web site of the Academy of Motion Picture Arts and Sciences found nothing. I'd tried the Web sites of the two films Aubrey had mentioned, *Appaloosa* and *Mimosa Magic*. They seemed to list the entire cast and crew down to the guy who swept out the set, but no Aubrey Andrews Armstrong or Montezuma Motion Pictures was mentioned.

Unfortunately, this didn't prove anything. Aubrey could go by "A. A. Armstrong." Or he could use a completely different professional name. And Montezuma Motion Pictures could have sold distribution rights or done some other tricky thing that made the name not appear on film credits.

Then I tried another tack, and discovered neither Aubrey Andrews Armstrong nor Montezuma Motion Pictures could be accessed anywhere in the country by the biggest telephone information site.

I wasn't ready to give up. I did the whole search of the motion picture sites again, this time using only the name "Armstrong." I found a bunch of people by that name, of course, but none of them was Aubrey or Andrews or anything else that sounded likely.

Things were not looking good for Aubrey, but it was all negative—lack of information didn't prove anything. I rested my head against my computer screen and wondered if I should quit.

Then it occurred to me that Aubrey's new production might have had some publicity around the state of Michigan, so I typed in "Michigan" and "film production." And the Michigan Film Office Web site came up.

"Yeah!" I said it aloud. "I can check with them. They ought to know about film activity all over Michigan."

Yes, there was an e-mail address. I fired off a query. Maybe that would get results.

What else could I do?

Getting some dinner seemed the best plan. I hid the notes I'd written on my fruitless search for Aubrey Andrews Armstrong, turned off the computer, got my jacket, and double-checked the lock on the street door. As I did, I peeked out and eyeballed the windows of the second-floor apartments across the street. Joe had recently signed a lease for one of them, and he'd spent nearly every evening over there painting. My conscience smote me; he was doing all this work because he wanted me to marry him and move in. And old dumb Lee couldn't make up her mind.

But that night, his windows were dark. I turned

on the shop's security light, then went out the back door. I zipped the jacket up; nights were already in the low forties in southwest Michigan. Pretty soon, I thought as I climbed into my old minivan, I'd get my annual yen for pumpkin bread.

Pumpkins. The thought of the orange veggie reminded me of Maia's uncle, Silas Snow, who had a fruit stand full of pumpkins. During the argument I had witnessed, Silas had referred to a business card, apparently left at his fruit stand by Aubrey. He'd said something about "sticking a business card under an apple."

That business card should have specific information about Aubrey. If I could get hold of it . . .

I turned the thought over idly, then checked my watch. Seven thirty. Aubrey had planned to pick up Aunt Nettie at seven, so the two of them, plus Vernon and Maia, should be at the Warner River Lodge by now. If I went out to Silas's, which I assumed was near the Ensminger place, there should be no danger of running into them. I turned the minivan toward Orchard Street.

Orchard Street was the quickest way to access the interstate highway and the Haven exit, where Silas's farm and his fruit stand were located. As I recalled the layout of the Snow property, the fruit stand was near the road, and a traditional white Midwestern farmhouse sat a hundred yards behind it. That simply had to be where Silas lived. Silas would still be up. And if I could convince him I wasn't a treasure hunter who was going to dig up his orchard, maybe he'd show me that card.

When I pulled into the fruit stand's parking area, my headlights swept over a sea of pumpkins. Who buys all those pumpkins? During each of the two autumns I'd spent in Warner Pier, these mass invasions of pumpkins had occurred. There were tiny

little pumpkins in baskets on the counters, wheel-
barrows full of medium-sized pumpkins, and hay
wagons loaded with giant pumpkins that needed a
forklift to move them into the trucks and vans of
buyers. There were rows of pumpkins marked "pie
pumpkins." There were washtubs full of pumpkins
marked "ornamental pumpkins." There were pumpkins with faces painted on them, pumpkins in arrangements with fancy gourds, pumpkins centering
decorations featuring weird squash.

I can understand cooking pumpkins for a few pies
and maybe some pumpkin bread. I can see making
Halloween and Thanksgiving table decorations out
of them. I can grasp using the larger ones to make
the front porch look seasonal, with country-flavored
arrangements of pumpkins and cornstalks and cutesy
scarecrows. I can visualize gigantic jack-o'-lanterns
made out of the largest pumpkins. But if every citizen of western Michigan did all those things, there
would still be pumpkins left over in the fruit stands.

My headlights showed that Silas Snow's fruit stand
was typical. It had a simple shed, open at the front
and sides, with three long tables where produce
could be displayed. There were baskets of apples
along the back wall, and a table loaded with winter
squash in the middle. But a majority of the space
was given over to pumpkins. Scads of pumpkins.
Oceans of pumpkins. Pumpkins galore.

There were so many pumpkins I couldn't find the
drive that led back to the house. I could see a light
on the porch and one inside the house. But I couldn't
figure out how to drive back there. I honked the
van's horn, thinking it might bring Silas out onto the
porch, but there was no reaction.

"I'll just have to walk," I said aloud. I dug my big
square flashlight out of the bin under the passenger's
seat, got out, and started picking my way through

the pumpkins. It was quiet, since Haven Road doesn't lead to anything but a bunch of summer cottages, and nearly all of those would be empty in mid-October. The interstate was only a few hundred yards away, true, but the trees still had enough leaves to hide the lights of the cars and trucks passing. The traffic sounds were loud, but the silence at Silas Snow's farm soaked them up like a blotter. I told myself that it wasn't really spooky, despite the way my imagination magnified every sound.

I had to keep the beam of the flash right where I was stepping, of course, since I didn't want to break either a pumpkin or my leg. This meant I was keeping my head down and concentrating on the ground right in front of my feet, but periodically I did a sweep of the pumpkin patch, planning a route.

I wasn't making very fast progress, but I eventually got around behind the fruit stand, with the building between me and the road. It was at that point that my flashlight swept over a huge heap of pumpkins. Some of them were smashed.

"Oh!" I guess I said it aloud. "The trespassers have been back!"

After seeing those broken pumpkins, I couldn't deny the spookiness of the situation. If Silas Snow was lying in wait for the treasure hunters who'd been trespassing on his property, I was in danger of getting hit by that shotgun blast he'd promised them. Or I might run into the trespassers themselves, and that wasn't a happy idea.

The Snow farm was not a good place to be in the dark, when neither Silas nor I could see what was going on. I decided I'd better wait until the next day to ask Mr. Snow for Aubrey Andrews Armstrong's business card. I began to turn around, ready to pick my way back through that sea of pumpkins and head for home.

But my flashlight's beam danced over something that wasn't round and that wasn't orange. It definitely wasn't a pumpkin. I moved the beam back to get a better look.

It was blue and oblong and it was sticking out of the heap of pumpkins. And there was something brown on the end of it. I had to concentrate for a long moment before my eyes made the object take a recognizable form.

It was the leg of a pair of blue jeans, and a brown workboot was sticking out the end of it.

"Scarecrow," I said, my voice a whisper. "It's got to be one of those scarecrows."

But what if it wasn't a scarecrow? I couldn't leave without making sure.

I tiptoed through more pumpkins, pushing some aside. Then I knelt beside the leg. I had to touch it. Thank God I was wearing gloves, I thought. Then I realized that was the dumbest thought I'd had in a long time. All I could touch was a boot.

I forced myself to reach out, and I nudged the boot. It moved, just a little. But it didn't move like a scarecrow's foot. It moved like a human foot attached to a very weak ankle.

I didn't scream, though I'm not sure why I didn't. I played the beam of the flashlight around, and now I saw something else sticking out of the heap of pumpkins.

It was a hand. A gnarled, dirty hand—the hand of a farmer who'd been working hard all his life.

Someone was buried under that heap of pumpkins.

Could that person be alive? I pulled my glove off, reached over, and touched the hand. It didn't respond to my touch, and it was cold.

I don't know if I smashed any pumpkins or not, but I ran all the way back to the van.

Chapter 5

Once in the van, I locked the doors then looked around inside to make sure nobody had climbed in while I was wading in pumpkins. The backward order of those actions indicated how rattled I was.

Luckily, just across the interstate, maybe three city blocks away, there was a gas station and convenience store. I drove across the overpass, nearly sideswiping a red Volkswagen with a Warner Pier High School bumper sticker in the rear window. It had pulled out suddenly from somewhere. The clerk in the bullet-proof booth called 9-1-1, and I waited there. The Haven Road exit is not in Warner Pier; the Warner County Sheriff's Department would be in charge of the situation. But they have a cooperative agreement with Warner Pier, I guess, because Jerry Cherry, one of the three Warner Pier patrolmen, was the first of-ficer on the scene.

I followed Jerry back to the Snow farm and parked on the edge of the fruit stand's gravel lot while law enforcement gathered. Sheriff's cars, Michigan State Police cars, and more Warner Pier cars pulled up, and all sorts of uniforms got out.

Jerry didn't make me show him where the body was; he found the spot from my description. After about twenty minutes, Chief Hogan Jones came over to my van, leaned on my door, and told me the sheriff said I could go home.

"We know where to find you, Lee," he said. "It's probably an accident anyway. We'll have to shift all those pumpkins before we know anything. What were you doing out here?"

I couldn't think of a good lie, so I told the truth. "I was trying to find out something about Aubrey Andrews Armstrong and his company. There was nothing on the Internet. I thought maybe I was spelling his name wrong, and since Silas Snow had mentioned having a business card . . ."

The chief shook his head. "You're incorrigible."

"I'm worried about Aunt Nettie."

"Then you'd better get home and be there when Armstrong brings her home."

He asked Jerry Cherry to follow me home. I assured him this wasn't necessary, but I was glad when he insisted.

As soon as I had gone into the house and had waved Jerry off, I discovered I was starving. Nerves, I guess. I had my head in the refrigerator checking the egg and English muffin situation when I heard another vehicle driving up. I wasn't mentally ready for Aunt Nettie and Aubrey, so I was glad when a glance out the side window showed me Joe's pickup. In fact, it was just plain good to see Joe, even though we had parted on bad terms.

I met him at the back door. "Do we have to settle the plans for the rest of our lives tonight?"

He smiled. He did have a wonderful smile. "Nope. Figuring out the rest of our lives is way too serious a subject for right now. How're you doing?"

"I'm okay. I guess the chief called you."

"He thought you might want some company."

"I could sure use a hug."

Joe obliged. "Have you eaten? I could take you out."

"No, thanks. I want to be here when Aunt Nettie gets home."

Joe frowned, but he didn't say anything.

"She *asked* me to be here, Joe. I was going to scramble myself some eggs. Do you want some?"

He gestured at the eggs and muffins on the cabinet. "I've had dinner, but I might have an English muffin and some of Nettie's peach jam."

"Preserves, you mean."

"Jam," he said. "And maybe sprinkle some pee-cans on top."

Joe and I carry on a joking argument about the proper names of items that are labeled differently in Texas and in Michigan, such as "preserves" versus "jam" and "pecahns" versus "pee-cans." He carries groceries home in a "bag," and I use a "sack." I'll let him settle the "Michigander" versus "Michiganian" controversy.

Joe split and buttered the muffins, then set the table with one place at the head and one on the side. I put on a large pot of coffee so Aunt Nettie could offer Aubrey some if she wanted to, then I scrambled eggs. Two of us moving around made Aunt Nettie's 1910 kitchen even narrower than it really is, but it was comforting to be doing homey things like scrambling eggs and toasting muffins and bumping rear-ends.

We didn't talk any more until we were sitting at the table in the dining room, and we kept the conversation light while we ate. I'd just finished rinsing the dishes when I heard an engine. Headlights flashed by the windows, and an SUV parked in the driveway. Our outdoor lights were on, so I saw Aubrey get out and go around to open the door for Aunt Nettie. Then he popped the rear end of the SUV and brought out Monte on his leash. The pup scrambled around in the bushes, undoubtedly giving them a good sprinkling, while Aunt Nettie and Aubrey stood talking. I couldn't make out words, but both of them sounded cheerful. Apparently the evening had gone well. I surprised myself by feeling pleased.

Joe and I retired to the living room, since the dining room overlooks the back door, and the back door is the one everyone usually uses. We didn't know if Aunt Nettie would want to say good-bye to Aubrey there.

But Aubrey came in with her. I heard their voices in the kitchen, then Aunt Nettie called out. "Hello! Do I smell coffee?"

"It may not be as good as the Warner River Lodge's," I said, "but it's there."

Monte frisked into the living room, pulling Aubrey along. Aubrey took the pup off his leash, and once again Monte bounced against my knees, then went to Joe. Joe greeted him, and Monte turned over, obviously ready to have his stomach scratched. He playfully kicked Joe with all four feet as Joe obeyed.

"Did you enjoy your dinner?" Joe asked the pup. "Or did you go along?"

"He went, but stayed in the SUV," Aubrey said. "I don't like to leave him in the kennel too long, though he's patient. But Nettie invited him in."

"There's nothing here a dog can hurt," Aunt Nettie said. I saw that she had put on a dressy blue pants suit. I don't think I've seen Aunt Nettie in a dress since Uncle Phil's funeral.

"I'm going to have a cup of coffee," she said. "Aubrey? Will you have one?"

"Yes, please." Aubrey beamed at her, then turned back to Joe and me as she went to the kitchen. "The restaurant is delightful. Wonderful food! The Lodge might be a great place to house part of our cast—if we're able to shoot here. Did you two have a pleasant evening?"

The question summoned up a mental picture of Silas Snow's boot sticking out from under that heap of pumpkins. I must have turned green, because Joe quit playing with the dog and reached for my hand. "Lee had a bad experience," he said. "We'll tell you about it after Nettie comes in."

Aubrey told Monte to stay, and the puppy lay down calmly. My nerves, however, began to jump wildly. I had just realized that I was going to have to explain the reason I'd gone out to Silas Snow's fruit stand, and I was going to have to explain it right in front of Aubrey.

Yikes! The truth might have done for Chief Jones, but it wasn't going to work now. It would not be tactful to tell Aubrey I'd been spying on him. What was I going to say?

Joe and Aubrey were chitchatting, and I was thinking madly. When Aunt Nettie brought in a tray with two cups of coffee and a dish of bonbons and truffles, I was ready. I don't like to lie, but I sure can sidestep.

"I'm on the Halloween Parade committee," I said, "and we have to round up a lot of punchers. I mean, pumpkins! So after I finished up at the office, I went out to Silas Snow's place. He's got loads of pumpkins." I turned to Aubrey. "The parade is a Chamber of Commerce function, and I'm on the body. I mean, the board! I'm on the chamber's board."

I stumbled on, telling about finding the hand and the foot sticking out from under the pumpkins. "It must have been Silas."

Aubrey's face screwed into a look of incredulous horror. "Are you sure he's dead?"

"Pretty sure," I said. I didn't describe the feel of his hand. "Of course, it might not be Mr. Snow. I couldn't see his face."

Aunt Nettie was looking concerned. "My goodness, Aubrey. Silas Snow is Maia's uncle."

Aubrey's eyes popped. "Not the one who owns the farm where *Love Leads the Way* happened?"

We all nodded.

"My God!" Aubrey appeared genuinely shocked. "Maia and I were out there this morning."

"Silas was angry with Maia. They had a big argument at the Rinkydink," I said.

Aubrey nodded solemnly. "She told me he was eccentric, warned me he might refuse to let us use the property."

"I'm surprised he let you on the place at all," Joe said.

"I guess Maia didn't ask permission. We didn't go to his house. We dropped by the fruit stand as we were leaving, but Maia said since his truck was gone, he must not be there. Maia drove us over there by some back road."

Joe nodded. "Maia probably knows every inch of the property, since it belonged to her grandparents. Besides, the place adjoins Ensminger's Orchards, where she and Vernon live."

"Did Maia marry the boy next door?" I asked.

Aunt Nettie shook her head. "No, both farms originally belonged to Mae's grandfather. Mae's mother died young, while her father was still alive, so Mae inherited that half of the family holdings. Luckily, Vernon was interested in farming it, so they just built a house and moved there."

"Does Silas have children?"

"I'm sure he never married."

"No children to speak of," Aubrey said. He chuckled. Joe and I smiled politely. Aunt Nettie looked puzzled, as if she didn't get the joke. It occurred to me that she was putting on an act; Aunt Nettie may look like a sweet, innocent lady, but she knows what's going on in the world, and I was sure she had caught Aubrey's feeble joke. I wondered what she was up to.

"Silas terrorized Warner Pier kids for fifty years," Joe said. "Not that we didn't deserve it."

"Why was that?" Aubrey asked.

"Snow's orchards were the equivalent of the local haunted house. The legend about the buried bank loot has been around since my mom was a girl—actually a lot longer. We always dared each other to go out there and dig for treasure. Then Silas would chase us off."

"He was threatening to get out his shotgun this afternoon," I said.

Aubrey's eyes got big. "I guess we were lucky to get off the place in one piece."

"I doubt he would have shot at Maia," Joe said.

"He might have if he'd known that—" Aubrey stopped talking in the middle of his sentence and took a drink of his coffee. We all stared at him, but he didn't seem to be planning to say any more.

"Known what?" I asked.

"Oh, nothing. Nothing at all." Aubrey answered in a way that made it obvious "nothing" meant "something."

I started to ask again, but Joe crossed his legs and managed to nudge my ankle in the process. His hint was pretty clear, though I didn't understand why he didn't want me to quiz Aubrey.

Aubrey turned his charm on Aunt Nettie. "Wonderful coffee and wonderful chocolates," he said. He pointed to the plate she'd brought out, almost touching a milk chocolate truffle. His effort to change the subject was transparent. "Now what's this one?"

"Coffee," Aunt Nettie answered. "A truffle covered and filled with milk chocolate that's been flavored with Caribbean coffee. The dark chocolate truffle next to it is Dutch caramel. According to our sales sheet, it's 'creamy, European-style caramel in dark chocolate.' It's a soft caramel—not like Kraft's."

Aubrey was looking entirely too innocent. "Do you ever make any peach or apple flavored chocolates?" he said. "TenHuis Chocolade is in the center of fruit country—or so I judge by my trip to Snow's farm and Ensminger Orchards."

"We make chocolates flavored with strawberry and raspberries," Aunt Nettie said. "I've never come up with anything mixing chocolate and apple that I thought was very tasty. And chocolate seems to overwhelm peach flavor."

"Maia mentioned that you do dipped fruits."

"Yes, but not peaches or apples."

Joe jumped back in the conversation. "How was Maia tonight? Still artsy?"

Aubrey frowned. "She was rather quiet."

"She was Mae tonight," Aunt Nettie said. "Really, it was a very nice evening. You're a perfect host, Aubrey, and Maia was quite her old self. You must have tired her out trotting around Snow's orchards."

"Did you take Monte out to Snow's?" Joe's voice was extremely casual.

"Yes. Of course, I had to keep him on his leash, but he enjoyed running around and doing a bit of digging. He—" Aubrey's voice came to an abrupt halt for a few seconds before he spoke again. "I promised Maia I wouldn't say anything."

We were back to what Aubrey and Maia had found at Snow's place. And I had the idea that Aubrey wanted us to ask about it, whether Joe thought we should or not.

"Okay," I said. "I'll bite. What did you and Maia find?"

Aubrey grinned. "Haven't you guessed?"

I hesitated, but Joe spoke up. "Buried treasure?"

"I'm afraid so." Aubrey produced the big, beat-up wallet—the one Monte had handed me that afternoon—from an inside pocket of his jacket.

"Where was it?" Joe said.

"Right near the old house, the one Dennis Grundy stayed in."

"Don't tell me it was buried in an old mayonnaise jar," Joe said.

Aubrey grinned. "I won't tell you that if you don't want me to, but it was. Actually an old fruit jar with a solid metal top. A cliché, I know. Maia kept the jar and most of the money."

Aubrey laid the wallet and the big bills out on the coffee table, and we all bent over it.

So Aubrey and Maia had found some money that might be part of the legendary bank loot supposedly buried by Dennis Grundy. This was very interesting. It also raised a lot of questions.

"My goodness," Aunt Nettie said. "That was a lucky find."

Joe spoke mildly. "That was an amazing find. You say it was right near the ruins of the old cottage?"

Aubrey nodded, very deadpan.

Joe grinned. "I could have sworn that—during the summer I was twelve—I dug over every square foot of the lot where that house is."

Aubrey grinned back and raised his eyebrows. "Yes, Maia and I were lucky. Of course, we had Monte to guide us. But it almost looked as if one of us knew right where to dig."

I interpreted this as meaning he thought Maia had buried the money herself.

Why? Why would she do that? Why would Maia bother to get hold of some of the old money, then bury it? She would have had to go to a coin and money collector or dealer for the money, then buy an old wallet. And an old canning jar.

I had to admit all those things would be easy to find in a casual crawl of Warner Pier antique shops. The money might be a little hard to locate, but the canning jar would be a cinch, and the old wallet wouldn't be too hard. The easiest part of all would be burying the treasure. But why bother?

That was a good question. Or I thought it was until I thought of a better one. I asked it. "Aubrey, what attracts you to Maia's novel? I mean, why make it into a film?"

"It's a compelling story," he said.

"Around Warner Pier, I'm afraid *Love Leads the Way* isn't considered great literature."

Aubrey laughed. "I'm afraid it wouldn't be considered great literature anyplace. But that's not the point. The point is that it could make a great movie."

"Why?"

"It's got everything: sex, violence, star-crossed lovers fighting obstacles to be together. An upbeat ending when Julia Snow leads Dennis Grundy away from a life of crime. And it's based on a true story."

"Is that important?" Joe said. "There are dozens of different versions of the Julia Snow–Dennis Grundy romance around here. Everything from 'It never happened' to 'Julia was no better than she should be before she ever met Dennis Grundy.' How do you know Maia's version is true?"

Aubrey thought a moment before he spoke. "Let's be frank. The script we finally come up with may not have much to do with Maia's book, and Maia's book may not have a lot to do with the real story. But to shoot this 'legendary' "—he traced quotation marks with his hands—"love story in the place where it actually occurred and to base it on a book by a niece of the heroine gives us a publicity hook that's hard to beat."

He gestured at the big bills and the wallet. "So if

the treasure we found is just stage dressing, so what?
I'm not going to look at it too closely."

"Does Maia understand that?" I asked.

"I think so. I hope so."

"She's sure caught up in the Hollywood gram-
mar," I said.

Aunt Nettie, Aubrey, and Joe all stared at me
blankly, and I finally realized what I'd said. "Glamour! I mean, she's caught up in the Hollywood
glamour!"

We all laughed, and Aubrey said he needed to be
getting back to his B&B. Joe and I cleared away the
coffee cups while Aunt Nettie waved good-bye to
him, then tactfully went to her room. Not that Joe
and I needed privacy. I certainly wasn't feeling romantic, and Joe didn't indicate he was either. I did
walk out to his truck with him, and he gave me a
good-night kiss before he left.

It was right in midsmooch, of course, that the
headlights hit us.

We moved apart, and I looked toward the car that
had pulled into the drive behind Joe's truck. The
headlights blinded me for a moment, but the driver
cut them off almost immediately, and I saw that it
was a Warner Pier police car. Chief Jones got out and
walked toward us.

"Lee, didn't see anybody around Snow's fruit
stand when you pulled in there, did you?"

"No. I didn't look for anybody, Chief. But it was
spooky and there were no lights at the stand, only
back at the house. Why?"

"Well, I guess we're going to have to get a complete statement from you tomorrow."

Joe gripped my arm. "What's wrong, Hogan?"

The chief scratched his head and looked more
craggy than usual. "When we finally got those
pumpkins off Silas . . . well, there was a big bash on

the back of his head. And a bloody shovel lying beside the body."

I gasped.

"Yep," the chief said. "Looks like somebody killed old Silas."

Chapter 6

It wasn't hard to get up the next morning, since I'd never closed an eye the night before. Besides, I knew I'd have to make a statement early in the day. Sure enough, Chief Jones was on the phone before I'd washed the breakfast dishes, asking me to come by his office.

The Warner County Sheriff had called in the Michigan State Police, I learned, and they were using the Warner Pier Police Department as headquarters for their investigation into Silas Snow's death. The detective in charge was Detective Lieutenant Alec Van-Dam. Lieutenant VanDam and I had crossed paths more than a year earlier, when another killing happened in Warner Pier. I'd met Joe because of that crime, but it hadn't been a pleasant experience. I'd just as soon have met Joe at a church social.

I headed down to meet Lt. VanDam. He still had a face like a peasant in a van Gogh painting, and he still had that straight, bright yellow hair that reminded me of a souvenir Dutch doll. He also still displayed that cool politeness that made me nervous.

There's no way of telling what's going on behind a polite façade like that. It's more chilling than yelling, snarling, or sarcasm.

I made my statement with only a few verbal faux pas. I did offer the information that I'd seen no sign of a "showman," when I meant a "shovel." But Van-Dam didn't keep me long; Chief Hogan Jones, who was still hanging around his own police station, was escorting me out the door by nine thirty.

Once we were outside I revealed my deepest wish to Hogan. "I don't suppose VanDam could arrange to arrest Aubrey Andrews Armstrong for homicide?"

Hogan grinned. "We'd all love for Silas to have been killed by an outsider, wouldn't we? And he might have been. But I'm afraid there's not much chance it was Armstrong. He's got a great alibi."

"Aunt Nettie?"

"Partly. But Sarajane Harding—you know, at the Peach Street B&B—was making cinnamon rolls and blueberry muffins in her kitchen from four p.m. until six forty-five. The kitchen overlooks her parking lot. She's willing to swear Armstrong's SUV never moved the whole time. In fact, for about a half hour he and the pup were in her backyard, having a training session."

"And she could see him all the time?"

"Right. He left at six forty-five, and Nettie says he got to her house at seven, right on the button. Not much time to stop and kill someone on the way."

I sighed and went to the office. The first thing I did, as usual, was check the e-mail. I was excited when I saw I had a reply from the Michigan State Film Office. I wasn't so excited after I read it. It was one of those notices that the e-mail recipient was away from her office for several days and would reply when she could.

Then I got a phone call from Tracy, asking about

the time of her appointment for a haircut. I fudged on that one. "I wasn't able to get hold of Angie last night," I said. I didn't explain I had forgotten to try. "I'll phone her right now."

"I got excused from English to call you," Tracy said. "I have play practice after school, but I'll try to call again after sixth hour. Or you could leave a message in the office."

I promised to do that, because her call reminded me of a bit of business I wanted to do at the high school. I wanted to ask Maggie McNutt why she had come into TenHuis Chocolade the afternoon before, very upset over something to do with Aubrey Andrews Armstrong. But Maia had come in, and I'd never gotten to quiz Maggie about just what upset her. I suspected that she knew something specific about Aubrey. I was curious. So an hour later I parked in the visitor's slot at Warner Pier High School and Junior High, locked my van, and headed for the front door with two notes in my pocket—one for Maggie and one for Tracy.

Warner Pier is a town of only twenty-five hundred, so our junior high and high school share an auditorium, cafeteria, and gym, with separate wings for the two levels of classes. The building is a standard red-brick, one-story model, with a driveway for buses on the south side. The office, administrative headquarters for both secondary levels, is right at the main door. A student helper took the note I'd written for Tracy—her haircut appointment was at five o'clock—then took the one I'd written for Maggie McNutt.

"I can put Mrs. McNutt's note in her box," the student said. "But if you want to talk to her, this is her free period."

"Good idea," I said. The student used the intercom to make sure Maggie was in her classroom, then told me which way to go, and I started down the indicated hallway toward the speech and drama classroom. But I'd gone only halfway when a voice behind me called my name. I turned to see Ken McNutt emerging from his classroom. He was as scrawny and colorless as ever, but his thin hair, usually oppressively neat, was ruffled.

He spoke abruptly. "Lee, do you know what's eating Maggie?"

"No." I spoke first, thought later. Maybe I shouldn't have admitted I knew anything was bothering Maggie. "She came by the shop yesterday, but we couldn't talk. Why do you think something's worrying her?"

"Maggie and I have known each other since we were the age of this freshman algebra class. We don't usually kid each other. When she begins to use drama techniques on me, I know she's upset."

"Have you asked her what's wrong?"

"Of course I have. She says it's nothing."

"Ken, I don't know a thing."

He snorted. "And if you did, you wouldn't tell me."

"That's what friends are for. But I might urge Maggie to tell you."

He kicked a locker. "Maggie has the attitude that she's going to protect poor old innocent Ken. She hates to give me bad news. But bad news is part of the deal for married people."

"Ken, I'm not getting in the middle of any communications problems you and Maggie may have."

"I know, I know. But she's such a good actress. . . ." Ken shook his head, kicked the locker again, then walked back into his classroom.

I felt sorry for any kid who whispered or passed a note that afternoon. Ken might appear meek and mild, but that day I thought he'd be happy to sentence any freshman who sassed him to a trip to the office and a hundred extra algebra problems.

When I got to Maggie's classroom, she looked as

unhappy as Ken had. A box of tissues was prominently displayed on her desk, and a couple of them had missed the wastebasket.

"Hidey, Maggie," I said. When I put on my Texas accent, it always makes Maggie smile, if not laugh, but this time that didn't work. "What's going on?"

Maggie shook her head and looked sadder than ever. She didn't say anything.

I pulled a student desk over close to her and squeezed all six feet of me into it. That didn't make her laugh either. "Okay," I said. "I want to know why you came in the shop yesterday and asked me if I were on speaking terms with Maia Michaelson."

Maggie shook her head, but she didn't say anything. So I asked another question. "And what do you know about Aubrey Andrews Armstrong?

"Oh, no!" Maggie finally spoke. Then she got up and closed the classroom door. "Lee, I'm in terrible trouble."

"What is it?"

"I can't tell you. I can't tell anybody."

"Even Ken?"

"Especially not Ken!"

I sighed. "Then I'll have to help you without knowing why you need help."

Big tears welled up in Maggie's eyes. "Lee, I . . ." She quit talking and reached for the tissues.

"What can I do, Maggie? Tell Maia to jump in the deep end of Lake Michigan?"

"I wish. I've got to warn Maia—I guess I've got to warn everybody—about that so-called Hollywood producer. But I don't know how to do it."

"How about saying something direct? 'Folks, this guy is a stranger. Don't give him any money until we can check him out.'"

Maggie's voice dropped to a whisper. "I don't need to check him out. I know he's a crook."

"Then tell Chief Jones."

"No! No! If I tell—well, Aubrey will tell."

I sat back in my desk. "Oh." Maggie and I stared at each other.

Whoops! So Maggie had some secret in her past, and Aubrey Andrews Armstrong knew what it was. I was speechless with surprise.

On the other hand, maybe I shouldn't be so surprised. The Maggie I knew was efficient and street-smart, the epitome of the gal who knew all the angles. And at thirty-five she'd outgrown the kid stage of her life. But no one is born street-smart. When Maggie was twenty and just as dumb as the rest of us were at that age, she had gone to Hollywood.

Whoops.

Maggie shredded her tissue. "I guess you've figured out that I . . . ran into him when I was in California."

My heart went out to her. And I felt a slight sense of—well, maybe it was pride. Pride that I was the one Maggie turned to when she needed a friend. I couldn't let her down.

"We were all young and dumb once, pal," I said. "You don't have to tell me about those creepy guys who hang around casting offices and beauty pageants. I understand. And, Maggie, I bet Ken would understand, too."

She shook her head violently. "No! Ken's good. He thinks I'm good, too. I just can't tell him I . . ."

A lot of Maggie's sentences were ending in the middle.

"Okay," I said, trying to sound brisk. "Recrimination time is over. Our problem is that Aubrey Andrews Armstrong is a crook, and we need to warn everybody in general, and Maia Michaelson in particular, about him. But we can't tell Maia exactly how we know he's a crook."

Maggie nodded.

"Well, through the magic of the Internet, I may have already solved this problem." I quickly outlined my efforts to check up on Aubrey the night before. "Anyway, he simply doesn't exist on the Internet. And I feel sure that the Michigan Film Office will either know about Aubrey or will know how to check him out. As soon as I can get in touch with the director there."

"After all the state budget cutbacks, I'm sure that's a one-person office, Lee. She's probably scouting locations. Or she could be in New York or California. It may be days before you can reach her."

"True. But in the meantime, I can hint to Maia that all is not right. And I can do it without mentioning you at all."

"Maia will never believe you. This is her dream come true."

I thought another moment. "Vernon! That's the answer. I can talk to Vernon. And nobody could ever suspect that Vernon will shoot his mouth off."

I guess Maggie and I might have hashed the matter over further, but the bell rang. Immediately students began to throng the halls and a group of them thronged into Maggie's classroom. Maggie tossed her tissue in the trash and took a deep breath. I made tracks.

As I paused outside the door, waiting for the crowd to clear, I heard Maggie inside. "Okay, people. Open your speech textbooks to page thirty-two. We'll start with the structure of the larynx." Her voice was clear, resonate, and confident. All traces of the fearful, tearful Maggie had disappeared. I thought of Ken describing her as "such a good actress." He was right.

I left the school and drove toward the shop. I had my assignment. Calling Vernon on the day after his wife's uncle had been murdered might be tricky. If

Silas had never married, as Aunt Nettie had said, Mae—I mean, Maia—might be the closest relative. Vernon might be closeted with the police or simply be incommunicado. But I vowed that I'd track him down.

As soon as I got to the office, I called the number listed in the Warner County phone book for Vernon Ensminger. A woman answered, using a hushed voice. When I asked for Vernon, she said he was at the funeral home. When I asked for Maia, the voice said she was resting.

I almost cheered. If Vernon was at the funeral home, and Maia was resting, I might have a chance to catch Vernon away from Maia. Since he followed her around like a puppy dog, this might be a onetime opportunity. I called the Warner Pier Funeral Home and asked if Vernon were still there. He was. I decided driving would be too slow. I ran the three blocks to the funeral home. Then I had to wait, since the receptionist said Vernon was conferring with the funeral director. I sat in one of the visitation rooms. Luckily, no one was in there to be visited. This gave me a few minutes to plan the angle I wanted to use to approach Vernon.

When I heard Vernon's voice rumble in the hallway, I emerged and waited discreetly until he and the funeral director had shaken hands and Vernon seemed to be moving in the direction of the front door. Then I spoke. "Vernon."

Vernon turned toward me. It seemed to take a moment for him to absorb just who I was. Then he gave a little gasp and came toward me.

I held a hand out in his direction. "I'm so sorry about Mae's uncle."

Vernon's giant hand enfolded both of mine. "Lee." His voice almost broke. "I'm so sorry you had to be the one who found Silas. I wouldn't have had that happen for the world."

"I didn't really see him, Vernon. I just saw enough to know I ought to call the police. Can I talk to you a moment?"

The funeral director unobtrusively waved us into the room he and Vernon had just left. It was more like a parlor than an office, but there was a writing table. Vernon and I took two easy chairs, and he waited for me to begin.

"Vernon, first, I hope you'll consider this conversation confidential."

"Sure, Lee. What's wrong?"

"Last night, after you and Mae went out to dinner with Aunt Nettie and Aubrey Andrews Armstrong, I decided to search the Internet and find out what I could about the movies Aubrey has made." I leaned forward. "Vernon, I found all sorts of movie sites, but the name Aubrey Andrews Armstrong was not listed on any of them."

Vernon dropped his head and stared at his feet.

I went on. "So I wondered if you knew any more about him."

"Such as what?"

"An address for his company, to begin with. For example, has he given you or Maia—Mae—a business card?"

Vernon shook his head.

"Did he write her a letter—something with a letterhead?"

"No. He phoned last week, then showed up over the weekend. She hasn't got anything in writing."

I sat back. "I'm worried about Aunt Nettie, of course. If he's not on the up-and-up, he could hurt her feelings, humiliate her. But I don't want to say anything to her if I'm wrong."

Vernon didn't say a word. He just dropped his head even lower. Apparently I wasn't going to get any verbal response.

"Vernon, if you have any more information about this guy—well, I could use it to search the Internet some more. Or to check with the Michigan Film Office. The director should know about any film company considering shooting in Michigan."

Vernon spoke then, but he kept his head down, and his voice was just a mumble. "I'll see what I can find out."

Neither of us moved, but we seemed to have said all there was to be said. Or I had. Vernon had hardly spoken at all. I stood up. "I don't want to smear Aubrey, then find out he's perfectly legitimate. But . . . I just don't see how he can be, Vernon. He mentioned several movies he'd supposedly been associated with. I went to the Web sites for those movies, and he's not listed anywhere. I tried the Academy of Motion Picture Arts and Sciences site. It lists hundreds of people who are in the film business. He's not among them. Anyway, if you find out anything, please let me know."

Vernon nodded again, and this time he stood up. "I'll ask Mae about it," he said. "But I won't tell her why I want to know."

He opened the door to the little conference room and stood back to let me go out. I thought he would follow me. But once I was out in the hallway, the door closed behind me. Vernon was staying in the conference room.

I turned around and stared at the door, surprised. And then I heard a sound from the other side of the door that was even more surprising.

Sobbing. Vernon was sobbing.

CHOCOLATE CHAT

AMERICA'S FIRST HEALTH FOOD?

As soon as the Spanish conquerors of the Mayas and Aztecs discovered chocolate, they began to rave about the healthfulness of the native American drink.

One widely-quoted conquistadore called the drink "the healthiest thing, and the greatest sustenance of anything you could drink in the world, because he who drinks a cup of this liquid, no matter how far he walks, can go a whole day without eating anything else."

Except maybe more chocolate.

European doctors of the sixteenth century still subscribed to many theories derived from the ancient Greeks, including the notion (proposed by famed second-century physician Galen) that all diseases and their cures were either hot or cold and moist or dry. Cacao was deemed "cold and moist" and thus was considered useful in curing fevers.

Mixing chocolate with spices and herbs, doctors warned, changed its efficacy; some spices made it good for intestinal problems, others turned it into an aphrodisiac.

Maybe they'd heard that Montezuma used to drink chocolate before he visited his harem.

Chapter 7

I walked back to the office slowly. The mental picture of Vernon Ensminger breaking into tears was hard to believe.

But why didn't I believe it? I was being stupid, I told myself. Vernon appeared stolid outwardly, but he still had feelings like anyone else. He'd been through a lot recently—his wife's complete personality change, the invasion of the movie producer, Maia's public quarrel with her uncle, then that uncle's murder. Even if he and Silas weren't close . . . I thought about that one for half a block. Vernon and Silas farmed neighboring property. They must have cooperated, maybe shared equipment. For all I knew they'd been bosom buddies.

Anyway, I'd given Vernon a broad hint about Aubrey, and he'd promised to help me find out more about the guy. And I hadn't had to bring Maggie into it. That was all I could do for the moment. Now I needed to concentrate on my own life, particularly my job.

My goal changed when I entered TenHuis Chocolade, however. My office had been taken over by Aubrey Andrews Armstrong. He was seated behind my desk having an interview with the local press in the person of Chuck O'Riley, editor of the *Warner Pier Weekly Gazette*. Monte was lying down at the foot of the desk.

Aunt Nettie was standing behind the counter in our little retail shop. "What are Aubrey and Chuck up to?" I asked her.

"Chuck wants to do a story about Aubrey's visit to Warner Pier. They set it up yesterday."

"I guess it's newsworthy. By Warner Pier standards, at least."

I could see Chuck leaning forward, apparently lapping up every word that dripped from Aubrey's silver tongue. I remembered my own reaction the night before, when Aubrey had spun his tale for Aunt Nettie, Joe, and me. I'd found myself wanting to believe him. And I remembered how Aunt Nettie had laughed, obviously flattered by his attention.

Then I thought about what Maggie had said about him: "If I tell, he'll tell." That was pure and simple blackmail.

Darn the man! Why couldn't he be legit? He was a charmer. I'd love to believe in him. But after my elementary investigations of him had turned up a suspicious lack of information, and after Maggie had reported knowing him in Hollywood—in a role she didn't want to become public or even private knowledge—I simply had to protect Aunt Nettie and Tracy and all the others who could be humiliated and hurt by him.

I steeled my resolution to resist Aubrey's charm with a Frangelico truffle. ("Hazelnut liqueur interior with milk chocolate coating, sprinkled with nougat.")

Chuck asked another question, grinning broadly. He was obviously happy with the story he was getting from Aubrey.

Chuck is the latest kid editor of the Warner Pier weekly. The newspaper always has a recent journalism graduate as an editor. A small paper, I suppose, draws newcomers or retirees to its staff. Anyway, Chuck was the only full-timer on the news staff. Three part-timers, all age sixty-plus, filled in the gaps, covering meetings and writing the occasional feature. One ad man and a publisher who also kept the books completed the workforce.

Chuck is five feet tall and five feet broad, a traditional Mr. Five-by-Five. He has dark hair and eyes that snap with interest at nearly everything. He also takes all the *Gazette*'s photos, and as I watched he produced his camera and gestured. I deduced that he wanted to take a picture to go with his story. Aubrey scooped up Monte and came out into the shop.

"Chuck wants to get a photo," he said. "I suggested that we include Monte and one of the real chocolate pups. If that would be all right with you, Nettie."

Aunt Nettie agreed, provided that the picture was posed so that the health department couldn't tell she'd had a dog in the shop. Chuck posed Aubrey, Monte, and a twelve-inch chocolate dog for a close-up. After a series of "Just one more" requests, he put his camera away.

"This has been a great interview, Mr. Armstrong," he said. "The *Gazette*'s readers are going to be fascinated with the plans you have to shoot *Love Leads the Way* here. Especially the part about the money."

Aubrey shook a finger at Chuck playfully. "I never claimed it was part of Dennis Grundy's treasure."

Chuck laughed. "I understand about the antique money. Actually, I was referring to the opportunity for investment."

"Please don't make too much of that. My major backers are likely to be in California."

Chuck turned to Aunt Nettie. "How about you, Mrs. TenHuis? Would you put money in Mr. Armstrong's project?"

Aunt Nettie smiled. "I haven't said no."

Her words sent my stomach into a nosedive. Aunt Nettie is far from wealthy, but she does have Uncle Phil's insurance money salted away. And she needs to keep it salted away in conservative investments to ensure a secure retirement for herself. An independent movie would be far too risky, even if the producer were honest.

Aunt Nettie patted me on the arm. "But I'd never do anything without consulting my financial advisor."

Aubrey and Chuck stared at me. Nobody spoke. Were they waiting for me to write a check? The silence lengthened.

They all apparently expected me to say something. So I did. "I'm only TenHuis Chocolade's business mangler—I mean, manager! I'm business manager for the company, not for Aunt Nettie. She handles her own finales. I mean, finances!"

I'd done it again. My twisted tongue had once again made me look and feel like a complete idiot. Aubrey tried to hide his snicker, but Chuck grinned broadly. Then he left.

I headed into my office, vowing to talk to Aunt Nettie about Aubrey as soon as he was out of the office. After all, if I was warning Maia about him, via Vernon, I owed as much to my own aunt. I sat at my desk, stared at my computer screen, and planned what I'd say and how I'd explain not telling her the night before.

But when Aunt Nettie popped her head into the office, Aubrey and Monte were still standing in the shop.

"Aubrey has invited me to go to lunch down at the Sidewalk Café," she said. "I shouldn't be too long."

She was beaming again. My heart turned over. I dreaded having to tell her Aubrey was a crook. I decided I could put off telling her for an hour. I knew her money was invested in mutual funds and CDs. She couldn't simply write Aubrey a check.

But the whole situation made me so jumpy that I almost fell out of my chair when the phone rang.

I was relieved to hear Joe's voice. "Have you had lunch?"

"No."

"I'd like to consult you about something, and I'm willing to trade a roast beef sandwich for an opinion."

"That's probably more than my opinion's worth. Actually, what I need is a sympathetic ear."

"I'm willing to throw that in. How about meeting me at the apartment in twenty minutes?"

"Your new apartment? Well . . . okay." I couldn't think of any excuse to avoid meeting Joe at his new apartment. It was all of two hundred feet away from TenHuis Chocolade. And I wasn't quite sure why I was reluctant to go.

I hung up, still feeling hesitant. Then it occurred to me that if Aunt Nettie was out to lunch I was supposed to be in the office. Of course, Hazel, her second-in-command, usually handled the lunch duty. I decided to check and make sure Hazel would be there.

I walked back to the workroom and discovered it was largely empty. Four people were at a table in the rear, wrapping Santas. Closer to the front Dolly Jolly was using a parchment cone to put dark swishes on the top of maple truffles.

"Hi, Dolly. Is Hazel here?"

"She's eating lunch in the break room!" Dolly spoke in her usual roar. "Do you need her?"

"No, I just wanted to make sure she was on the premises before I went to lunch. I see they've got you decorating. I could never learn to do that."

"It's just a matter of practice! I learned on my first job! In an ice cream shop!"

"What did you do? Add the curls to the tops of cones?"

"Ice cream cakes! They were our specialty!" She flourished the cone of dark icing and another graceful curve appeared on top of another milk chocolate--covered truffle. "I can write 'Happy Birthday' in any kind of script!"

I laughed and turned to go, but Dolly cleared her throat, a noise something like a bull elephant's trumpet. Then she did something really odd. Odd for Dolly, that it. She whispered.

"That Maia Michaelson—what do you think of her?"

"She's not my best friend," I said cautiously. "What do you think of her?"

"She was only interested in that movie guy. I'd like to talk to her, but it wasn't a good time." She was still whispering. "I was interested in how she writes."

"Oh, yes! You're an author, too."

Dolly got redder than usual and forgot to whisper. "Just nonfiction! All about food! I could never write fiction!"

I leaned a little closer. "Your manuscript was a lot more fun to read than Maia's novel!"

Dolly spoke again, and this time she remembered to drop her voice. "I thought the book was a dud, too. But the family background . . ." She frowned. "The Snows . . . are they . . . well, respectable?"

"You'll have to ask Aunt Nettie. There aren't many of them. As far as I know, Maia's the only quirky one. And I think the book has just gone to her head. She'll probably come down to earth sometime soon. Of course, Silas was a bit crotchety."

I told Hazel I was leaving, then I left. I didn't understand Dolly's interest in Maia's novel, but I wasn't worried about it. I was more concerned about why I was so reluctant to meet Joe for lunch in his new apartment.

Joe was lucky to have that apartment. Warner Pier's quaintness has made the town so darn popular that it's almost impossible for anybody but a millionaire to buy or rent a place to live. That was one reason Joe had spent the past three years living in a room at his boat shop. I think he'd been perfectly comfortable there with his hot plate, microwave, TV set, and rollaway bed until I'd come on the scene. I didn't object to his Spartan living arrangements, but he was so self-conscious about them that he refused to invite me over for more than a pizza. Since I lived with Aunt Nettie in an old house that offered little privacy, Joe and I had been hard put to find someplace to be alone together. And we liked to be alone together sometimes, now that we were engaged. Or on the verge of being engaged. Or going steady. Or whatever our relationship was.

I was almost thirty, and Joe was past it. We'd both been through unhappy marriages and had come out the other end, and Joe was eager for us to set a wedding date. So far I'd been dragging my feet, though I wasn't sure just why. I suspected that Joe thought getting a decent place to live would be an inducement for me to make that final decision and commit marriage.

But he hadn't been able to find anything in his price range until Warner Pier's summer rush was over. He couldn't afford to buy a house, and between Memorial Day and Labor Day every apartment in town is occupied either by tourists, by summer people, or by temporary help—the teachers, college students, and others who staff Warner Pier's restaurants, bed and breakfast inns, motels, and marinas during the tourist season. It had been September fifteenth before Joe signed a lease on a second-floor apartment overlooking Warner Pier's quaint Victorian main drag, Peach Street.

The apartment had two bedrooms, a nice kitchen, and a large living room. The drawback was that it had been thoroughly trashed by four college students who had rented it all summer. Joe got a month's rent free by offering to clean and repaint himself. So for the past three weeks he had spent all his free evenings working over there, and I'd helped him on a lot of them.

But lately he'd been pressing me harder and harder about setting a wedding date. But since I'd found Silas Snow's body, he hadn't mentioned Aunt Nettie or getting married at all. As I crossed the street toward the new apartment, I hoped he'd continue that policy.

The apartment's entrance was a door between a gift shop and an art gallery. It was unlocked. I went inside, then called out as I went upstairs. "It's me!"

"Come on up!"

Joe was in the newly painted kitchen. He had set the secondhand maple table he'd acquired with his two plastic place mats. I happened to know he'd scrounged them from his mother; they were patterned with blue checks. A sack from the Sidewalk Café sat in the middle, and he was pouring a Diet Coke.

"Roast beef with horseradish sauce," he said. "On thin rye."

"Yum, yum. All that and a dill pickle."

Joe shared out the sandwiches (his was ham and swiss) and piled chips in the middle of the table.

"I guess I'm starving," I said. "I don't remember much about breakfast."

"I've got a package of Oreos, if you want dessert."

We ate in silence for ten minutes, and it was comforting. As Joe swallowed his last bite of ham and cheese, he poured more Diet Coke. Then he finally spoke.

"Still upset about Silas?"

"Not for the past hour or so. I haven't had time to think about it."

"Something new?"

"Well, yeah." I chewed, swallowed, and decided I still wasn't sure what to tell him about Aubrey. "But you said you needed advice."

"I need your opinion on some tile for the bathroom."

"Tile? You're putting new tile in the bathroom? I thought the landlord said he wouldn't replace the tile in there, since it's not cracked or anything."

"I'll buy it myself. You said you didn't like green."

"My opinion doesn't count."

"Sure it does. I don't want to get something that will drive you crazy." He got up and brought a small box over to the table, then pulled out several pieces of ceramic tile. "I tried to get light colors. Do you like the pink? The white? The light blue? Or do you want to go for the fifties look with the oatmeal fleck?"

"I don't want to pick out tile for somebody else's apartment."

Joe's jaw tightened, and his eyebrows got that thundery look that means he's mad. He dropped the tile back into the box and stood up. "That remark makes your intentions pretty plain."

"What does that mean?"

"It means I want to get married, and you don't. At least not to me."

"The bathroom tile tells you that?"

"Well, calling this 'somebody else's apartment' makes it pretty plain you don't think you'll ever live here."

"I don't know that! I just—oh, we've been over

this before. I botched things so badly the first time. You know how I feel."

"I'm beginning to think I do."

"Joe, I didn't come over here to make a plan for the rest of my life!"

"Why did you come?"

"You invited me to lunch. Plus I'm just a weakling. I'm upset about Aunt Nettie and I wanted a shoulder to cry on."

"What's wrong with Nettie?"

"Oh, she's gone out to lunch with this nutty guy who claims he's a movie producer."

"So? I thought the chief told you not to worry about that."

"How can I help it? Joe, I know he's a crook."

"How do you know?"

I left out any reference to Maggie, of course, as I sketched for Joe my Internet search and its lack of results. It was better than talking about bathroom tile and all its implications.

"And now he's talking to her about investing in this supposed movie he claims to be making."

Joe grinned. "Lee, you're perfectly right to be concerned, but you really don't have to worry about Nettie."

"I know she's no dummy! I'm not worried about her losing her money! I'm worried about her losing her— her pride. Her self-respect. I'm worried about her friends laughing at her. I'm worried that if a really nice guy comes along, she'll be afraid he's just trying to exploit her like Aubrey the creep."

Joe was grinning more broadly. He took my hand. "Lee, you're a sweetheart. But you really don't need to worry about—"

A loud rapping sounded, and Joe quit talking in the middle of his sentence.

"Is that someone downstairs? At the door?" I asked.

I followed as Joe walked through the living room and threw up one of the windows that overlooked the street. The screens were off, so he stuck his head out. "Hi, Nettie."

I put my head out, too. Aunt Nettie, Aubrey, and Monte were on the sidewalk below, looking up at us.

"Come on up," Joe said.

"You come down," Aunt Nettie said. "Aubrey's offered to take me out to see the site of the big romance, the cottage where Dennis Grundy courted Julia Snow. I knew you wanted to see it, too, Lee. Why don't the two of you come with us?

Chapter 8

"Vernon said it would be all right," Aunt Nettie said. "I haven't been out there in years."

Aunt Nettie was sounding a bit urgent. I concluded that she wanted someone to go with her. I agreed; I didn't want her wandering off to remote spots alone with Aubrey. Not after what I'd been told by Maggie.

To cinch the deal, Joe spoke. "I'd like to go. I've never been out there when I wasn't trespassing."

Ten minutes later Joe and I had cleared away our lunch debris and were waiting on the sidewalk when Aubrey pulled his SUV up in front of Joe's apartment. As we got in, Monte gave us a welcoming bark from his heavy plastic traveling crate in the rear deck.

"Chuck O'Riley wanted to shoot some pictures out there," Aubrey said. "He interviewed Vernon at the police station for his news story on Silas's murder, and at the same time he asked if he could take some pictures at the cottage. Newsmen are nervy! I almost thought he was going to ask Maia to come along. I wouldn't have had the courage. Chuck's going to meet us there."

"If Vernon gave Chuck permission then Maia must be Silas's heir?" I asked.

"If Silas had a will, I'm sure it hasn't been read," Joe said. "But Vernon seems to be in charge at the moment. You can't just ignore a farm until the courts act. Somebody has to make sure the stock is fed and the garden watered. It would be normal for a neighbor, especially one who's a relative, to step in."

For once Aubrey didn't have much to say. In fact, we all grew quiet as we reached the Haven Road exit and turned toward Silas Snow's fruit stand. The area was still marked off by police tape, and one lone sheriff's deputy was stationed there. We went west on Haven Road, then turned south when we reached Lake Shore Drive, maybe two-tenths of a mile west of the interstate.

The cottage was at what might be considered the back of Silas Snow's property, since his house was near the interstate. The one-lane road that led to the cottage was less than a mile south of Aunt Nettie's house, which is on the inland side of Lake Shore Drive. The Grundy cottage lane also turned inland off Lake Shore Drive, and the house wasn't far off the road. I'd been by there dozens of times, but the area was so overgrown that I'd never realized any sort of structure was behind the trees and bushes.

"The cottage isn't much to look at," Aubrey said, "but the historical context makes it interesting."

I thought "historical context" was a pretty fancy term for "rented by minor gangster for three months seventy-five years ago," but I kept my mouth shut.

After Aubrey pulled into the sandy drive, we all sat in the SUV and surveyed the cottage. I'd been expecting Dennis Grundy's old cottage to be a ruin, but it wasn't. It wasn't in the best repair, but it was a sturdy little Michigan cottage of the type built around 1920. An ancient coat of white paint still clung to the siding, and rusted screen wire surrounded what had been a sleeping porch where the frame of an old metal cot stood at one end.

The vegetation apparently hadn't been cleared in several years. It was thinner around the house than near the road, but saplings were growing next to the foundation and the grass and weeds in the yard were high. Trees hung thickly above the cottage, and its roof was speckled with patches of moss. It looked lonely and uncared-for, but it wasn't falling down.

"I'd have expected Silas Snow to sell this place," Joe said. "The house isn't worth anything, but the lot is. Walking distance to the lake, after all. It should bring a good price."

"Snow apparently continued to rent the cottage to vacationers up until about ten years ago," Aubrey said. He got out of the SUV, and the rest of us followed his lead.

"It's spooky," I said. "Somehow I wouldn't be surprised if Dennis Grundy's Model A came chug-chugging down the drive."

Aunt Nettie gave a nervous laugh, but before she could hit her third "hee-hee," I heard a strange sound. I clutched Joe's arm and gasped.

It was the chug-chug of an old motor.

Joe laughed. "I believe you summoned up Dennis Grundy's ghost, Lee. Or at least the ghost of his car."

"What is it?"

"I think," Joe said, "that it's actually a Volkswagen."

And sure enough, a red Volkswagen came down the lane from behind the house. It was a real, antique Volkswagen, not one of the new ones. And behind the wheel was Ken McNutt. He stopped when he saw us. The VW was nose to nose with Aubrey's SUV.

Aunt Nettie, Joe, and I all laughed and waved. "I'll have to move the SUV so he can get out," Aubrey said. He got behind the wheel again and backed out onto Lake Shore Drive.

Joe spoke to Ken. "What are you doing here?"

"Oh, I had an hour's break, and I wanted to see this place." Ken nodded toward the cottage. "This is the site of Maia Michaelson's big romance novel, isn't it?"

Joe's voice was curious. "How'd you find it?"

"The high school custodian drew me a map," Ken said. "And now I've got to hurry, or I'll be late for a parent conference."

He drove on out the lane and waved to Aubrey. The VW gave a cheerful beep-beep as it turned onto Lake Shore Drive.

"I'd forgotten that Ken McNutt is a VW hobbyist," Joe said. "I understand he has four of them. At least two are in driving condition."

I stared after Ken. His Volkswagen was shiny and cared-for. It might have come straight off a production line of the late 1950s. The only modern thing about it was the Warner Pier High School bumper sticker in the back window.

Why did that seem familiar?

I caught my breath. I'd seen a red Volkswagen like that one. The night before, right after I discovered Silas Snow's body, I'd pulled out onto Haven Road in a big hurry. And I'd nearly rear-ended a red VW with a Warner Pier High School bumper sticker in the back window. The sticker hadn't been on the bumper. It had been inside the back window, just the way Ken's sticker was, the way people who are picky about their cars' finishes display bumper stickers.

I hadn't gasped loudly, but Joe had heard me. "What's wrong?" he asked.

"Nothing," I said. "I just remembered a prone

call—I mean, a phone call! I forgot to call the bank. I'll do it when I get back to the office."

We walked toward the house, but my mind was racing. Was it Ken McNutt's VW that I'd seen the night before, close to Silas Snow's fruit stand? Right after Silas was killed?

If it had been, who had been driving? Ken? Or Maggie? Or was there another red Volkswagen in Warner Pier with a high school bumper sticker in the back window? After all, I hadn't bothered to look at the license plate.

And why hadn't I wanted to tell Joe I'd seen it there? The answer to that one wasn't hard. If I told Joe right at that moment, I'd probably have to tell Aubrey. And I didn't want to tell Aubrey anything that might involve Maggie.

I realized Joe was looking at me closely. He had said something, and I hadn't even heard it. I pulled my mind back to my surroundings. Whatever the reason for the VW being near Snow's fruit stand, I had to forget the whole thing and concentrate on the current moment. I'd decide what to do about the Volkswagen—if anything needed to be done—later.

By the time I gathered my thoughts, Aubrey had parked the SUV again and had taken Monte out of his crate. He pushed a fancy metal stake into the sandy earth near the corner of the cottage and hooked Monte to it by a long leash. I decided Aubrey must have the back of the SUV packed solid with puppy equipment.

Monte seemed content to frisk about, sniffing around under the bushes. Joe, Aunt Nettie, Aubrey, and I began to prowl in much the same way, peeking in the uncurtained windows of the house.

"I don't have a key," Aubrey said.

"I don't think there's anything inside but a thick layer of dust," Aunt Nettie said. "We certainly don't need to go in."

The cottage originally had only two rooms, or so I guessed. There was a living room, with a kitchenette separated from it by a counter, and there was a bedroom. A bathroom now opened off the bedroom, but the fixtures and linoleum were forties-style. And the bathroom stood on piers made of cement blocks. The main part of the house had a solid foundation.

The views through the windows revealed only a few sticks of furniture, and they all looked too modern to have been used by Dennis Grundy.

"I'm sure this place didn't have indoor plumbing when Dennis Grundy rented it," Aunt Nettie said. "The kitchen appliances and that counter you can eat at were added later, too. At least, I never saw a counter like that in a really old house."

"The hole where the pipe from the wood stove would have been is still there," I said. "Up there in the corner."

"It wouldn't have been a bad little cottage for a cheap vacation," Joe said. "In the twenties lots of people still had outdoor plumbing and wood stoves."

"It would have been like camping." I gestured at the metal cot frame on the porch. "The porch might have been a really nice place to sleep. If you had plenty of blankets."

"Where did you and Maia find the money buried?" Joe asked.

"Around behind the house." Aubrey led the way to a little pile of dirt.

"That's probably where the old fence corner would have been," Joe said. He pointed to a stick of wood and a bit of wire. "At least, that looks like the remnants of a wire fence."

"Did you say the money was in a mayonnaise jar?" Aunt Nettie wanted to know.

Aubrey laughed. "I know that's a cliché. . . ."

"What else would Dennis have had to bury money

in?" Aunt Nettie said. "Maybe a syrup tin. But he would have had to use something he could get hold of easily."

"Burying the money has always sounded crazy to me," I said. "Why? Why would he bury money anyway? How much was in the jar?"

"Just about a hundred dollars," Aubrey said.

"That wasn't much loot from a bank job, even in 1930. And why was the wallet buried with it? It doesn't make sense."

Joe answered. "It makes sense if the wallet was just stage dressing for the antique money."

Aubrey grinned. "I didn't say that. That's strictly *your* idea, Joe."

We kept wandering around, with me keeping a careful lookout for poison ivy, until another car pulled in and Chuck O'Riley got out.

Aubrey went to meet him, sweeping off his wide-brimmed hat, and Monte barked a greeting. Chuck shook hands with Aubrey, but then, to my surprise, he came toward me. "Lee, I want to talk to you."

"What about?"

"About finding Silas Snow's body. When I saw you earlier I didn't realize you were the one who found him."

I guess I stared. We all took the Warner Pier *Gazette* for granted as a source for local news. But Warner Pier news rarely included crime. The *Gazette* was where I caught up on the school board meeting or the zoning commission. Or about visitors who claimed to be movie producers. I didn't expect to read about murders there. I'd forgotten Chuck would be writing up Silas Snow's murder, even though Aubrey had mentioned Chuck's interviewing Vernon earlier.

I gathered my thoughts and answered Chuck's questions as briefly as I could. I definitely slurred over my reasons for going to the Snow fruit stand in the first place, of course. And I tried to be matter-of-fact about finding the body.

"At first," I said, "I thought the hand and foot must belong to a scarecrow."

"What made you realize it was a body?"

The recollection of how that foot had wiggled sprang into my mind, and I couldn't answer. I put my hand over my mouth and shook my head.

Joe moved in and put his arm around me. "I think that's enough, Chuck."

But I couldn't let Joe protect me. I tried to speak. "I knelt down," I said. "I troweled—I mean, I touched! I touched the boot. It didn't move like a scarecrow's boot would move."

"What did you do then?"

"I ran through those pumpkins like a friend. I mean, a fiend!" I stopped and took a deep breath. "I ran like hell, Chuck."

That seemed to settle Chuck's curiosity. He thanked me and moved on to Aubrey, posing him on the porch of the cottage.

I guess I was still a bit shaken; I wanted to get away from Chuck before he thought of any more questions. So I walked away, following the sand lane further, toward wherever Ken McNutt had been. Joe followed me.

To my surprise, the bushes and trees behind the cottage thinned out quickly.

"What's back there?" I said. Joe and I walked about a hundred feet and came out in an apple orchard.

"McIntosh?" I said.

Joe touched one of the hanging apples. "Looks more like Jonathan."

"I guess we've reached the active part of the Snow farm."

The trees weren't too large. Fruit farmers, I've

come to realize, don't want their trees to get very tall. They're easier to prune, spray, and pick if they're shorter and wider.

This orchard stretched on for a long way, hundreds of trees marching along in straight lines, forming squares and rectangles and diamonds. The ground beneath them, of course, was cleared. Most growers mow around their trees. I wasn't sure why.

Joe was a native of orchard country. I turned to him. "Why do fruit farmers mow around trees?"

"Most of them believe tall grass takes nutrients from the trees. Besides, they want to keep the area smooth and even so they can run tractors and trailers down the rows without bouncing fruit around and bruising it."

Now, in October, the fruit trees were still a dull green, but the oaks and maples—the woods around edges of the orchard—were turning brilliant reds and oranges.

"It is beautiful," I said.

"Silas was a good grower," Joe said. "Everything looks neat. Spic-and-span. The only thing I see is one ladder out of place."

He gestured, and I saw it, too. A three-legged ladder, the kind used for picking fruit, was standing beside a tree. But it wasn't an apple tree. It was a taller maple at the edge of the orchard.

"Lee! Joe!" Aunt Nettie's voice came from behind us.

"I guess she's ready to go," Joe said.

"So am I."

We called out, then made our way back down the lane and into the yard of the cottage. Aubrey was pulling up Monte's stake. Aunt Nettie was holding the long leash, and the puppy immediately made for the bathroom "wing," pulling Aunt Nettie behind. Monte crawled under the bathroom, finding an easy path between the cement blocks that held the room up. He began digging around in the sandy dirt.

"Come on, Monte!" Aubrey sounded exasperated. "You'll get mud in the car."

He took the leash and hauled the pup out, over Monte's loud objections. As predicted, the dog was a mess, his chocolate hide covered with gray dirt. Joe held him by the collar while Aubrey brought a towel and a brush—more puppy gear—from the SUV and cleaned him up. Then he led Monte over to the vehicle, opened the rear end, and spoke to the puppy. "Kennel, Monte."

Monte jumped right up, leaping into the SUV and going into his big carrying case.

Aubrey was rewarding him with a dog snack when the shot rang out.

Chapter 9

I think I was more conscious of a metallic *clunk* than I was of the shot. Which was logical, I guess. The sound of the shot being fired didn't have a lot of significance. The shooter could have been firing in any direction.

But that *clunk* was proof that the shot had hit the SUV. The guy with the gun was firing in our direction.

We all yelled at the same time.

"Get down!" That was Joe.

"Aunt Nettie! Duck!" That was me.

"Heavens! Was that a shot?" That was Aunt Nettie.

"What the hell?" That, of course, was Aubrey.

Monte even began to bark.

The next second the four of us had ducked behind the passenger side of the SUV. Aubrey had to have gotten around, over, or under the vehicle's open rear door, and I've never been sure how he did it. But he did. He was right there with the rest of us, cowering.

Nothing else happened for a long moment. Monte

gave one last howl and quit barking. We all looked at each other. None of us seemed to have any idea of what to do next. The moment stretched. No more shots came. Finally Joe spoke. "I don't have my cell phone."

"I don't, either," Aubrey said.

There was another minute of silence before Joe spoke again. "If we had a stick, we could hold Aubrey's hat up and see if it draws fire, I guess."

Aubrey gave a weak laugh. "Just like a B western."

"It worked for Clint Eastwood."

We huddled a few more minutes.

"I don't hear anybody moving around in the bushes," I said.

"I think that was a rifle shot," Joe said. "A guy with a rifle doesn't have to be close. He's just got to be able to see through the bushes and trees."

Aunt Nettie came up with a practical plan, as she usually does. "Do you think we dare open the doors on this side of the SUV and get in?"

"Let's try it," Joe said.

Aubrey opened the right front door. Nothing happened. He started to climb in, but Joe stopped him. "That shot seemed to be aimed at you," he said. "You stay down. Let me drive. At least you've got tinted windows."

I wasn't sure the tinted windows were useful. The guy with the rifle wouldn't be able to see who was in the driver's seat, true, but he was bound to figure out someone was. He might think it was Aubrey and shoot Joe by mistake.

But Aubrey didn't argue, and I didn't, either. Joe got in, followed by Aubrey, who slid in and crouched with his knees on the floor and his elbows in the front passenger seat. I opened the door to the rear bucket seats, and Aunt Nettie and I got in, taking the same prayerful position.

"The back's still open," Aubrey said.

"Can it be closed from inside?" Joe asked.

"I don't think so."

"I can close the kennel," I said. I reached around my seat and did it. At least Monte couldn't jump out.

"Good," Joe said. "I'll back out and drive off gently. As soon as we're a little way up the road, I'll get out and close up."

The plan worked. Joe backed the SUV out onto Lake Shore Drive. Monte barked, maybe trying to tell the stupid humans the rear door was still open. Joe shifted into drive and moved forward, driving slowly for about a quarter of a mile before he stopped. Aubrey started to open his door, but I stopped him. "No, Aubrey. You stay down." I jumped out, slammed the rear door, and was back inside in less than five seconds.

When we moved off again, Joe gunned the motor and dug out. And we all took deep breaths.

"Go to my house," Aunt Nettie said. "We can call the sheriff from there."

That gave me nearly a mile to try to absorb what had just happened.

First, why had we all assumed Aubrey was the target of the man with the rifle?

That was easy. Aubrey had been at the back of the SUV. Joe, Aunt Nettie, and I had all been around on the passenger's side, ready to get into our seats. The shot had come from the driver's side of the SUV. Aubrey was probably the only person the gunman could have seen clearly enough to aim at.

Besides, I admitted to myself, after what Maggie had told me, I was ready to kill Aubrey myself. It was easy to assume that someone else had a reason. Maggie sure did.

At that thought, my heart leaped to my throat, then dropped to the pit of my stomach. I didn't want to involve Maggie in this. But Ken had actually been out in the area. Maybe Maggie had been there, too. Ken was worried about Maggie; he'd told me as much that morning. If she'd told him that Aubrey had threatened her . . . I shoved the idea out of my mind. I didn't want to believe Ken or Maggie could be involved. Besides, how could they have known Aubrey would be there?

Joe pulled into Aunt Nettie's drive, and Aunt Nettie got out her house keys. "That cottage is outside the city limits," she said. "I'll call the sheriff."

"No, wait!" Aubrey's voice was sharp. "I'm beginning to think we're overreacting to this whole episode."

"Aubrey! Someone shot at you!"

"I'm sure it was some sort of accident."

"Even if it was, you can't simply allow people to fire around wildly without complaining about it."

"But why would anybody want to shoot me?"

"Why would they want to shoot any of us?" Joe said. "Let's see if we can find the bullet hole."

We all got out and looked. The bullet hole was high up on the SUV, right at the back, where the roof met the side. Joe got Aubrey to restage the shooting, to stand right where he'd been when the shot rang out. Then he whistled softly. "Aubrey, that guy didn't miss you by six inches."

Aubrey looked a little green, but he stuck to his argument. "It must have been some sort of accident."

"I guess the guy saw the outback hat and thought you were a kangaroo," I said. "Are we going to call the cops or not?"

Joe hesitated, to my surprise, and Aubrey carried the day. Or at least a compromise was reached. Joe said he and Aubrey could drive Aunt Nettie and me back to town, then show the SUV to Chief Jones privately. They'd tell him what had happened without going through the county dispatcher. Maybe, since the dispatcher wouldn't be using the radio to send out a patrol car, we could keep the report quiet.

I thought it was screwy, but Joe was, after all, a lawyer. He was even Warner Pier City Attorney. If he thought that was good enough, I wasn't going to argue. I'd spent enough of my day making statements and being quizzed by detectives. But knowing that some unknown rifleman was prowling around on the Snow farm less than twenty-four hours after its owner had been beaten to death seemed highly suspicious to me.

The SUV was the only vehicle available, so Aunt Nettie and I accepted a ride back to TenHuis Chocolade. As I got out of the SUV, I did reach behind the seat to give Monte's chocolate-colored hide a pat.

The first thing I saw as I walked in the door was more dark chocolate puppies. Dolly Jolly was standing at a big worktable in the front of the shop, molding them.

"Oh, hi!" she said. As usual, Dolly's voice was loud enough to shatter glass. "Lindy Herrera came by to see you, Lee!"

"Did she say what she wanted?"

Dolly didn't answer for a long moment. She was pouring molten dark chocolate into a mold that made a dozen one-inch dogs. The mold was arranged something like an ice tray and Dolly was carefully filling each compartment with melted chocolate she ladled from a big stainless steel bowl at her elbow. This is one of the first jobs Aunt Nettie gives new employees. It looks easy, but when you're learning, it's best to concentrate, and Dolly was doing that. I could tell by the way she was sticking her tongue out.

She put her ladle in the bowl, then tapped the mold gently on the table to remove any air bubbles.

Next she picked the mold up and ran a spatula across the top, scraping any excess chocolate back into the bowl. Then she looked up at me and spoke. "All Lindy said was that she'd heard a juicy bit of gossip! But she didn't offer to tell it to me! Said she'd wait for you!"

"A juicy bit of gossip. Hmm. I'll give her a ring."

But first I had another job to do. I'd put off telling Aunt Nettie about Aubrey's lack of credentials as long as possible. I couldn't tell her what Maggie had said, but I needed to tell her at least as much as I had told Vernon.

I turned to her. "Aunt Nettie, could you come in the office a minute. There's something I need to discuss with you."

Aunt Nettie sighed. "Can we put it off? Lee, I should make a condolence call on Maia and Vernon. Can you come with me?"

I must have frowned, because she went on. "After all, I was out to dinner with them last night. I guess I could go alone." She sounded doubtful.

"No, I don't want you to do that," I said. "I'll give Lindy a quick call, then go with you. We can talk when we get back. Do we need to take food?"

"Maybe a plant would be better. We can stop at the Superette."

Maybe I was looking for an excuse not to tell Aunt Nettie about Aubrey. Anyway, I put it off.

Lindy wasn't in her office, so I left a message, and Aunt Nettie and I left on a condolence call I'd rather be shot than make.

Come to think of it, I nearly had been shot. A shiver ran around my shoulders and down my back. Then we got in my van and headed back the way we'd gone earlier, turning off the interstate at Haven Road. Only this time we turned inland, away from Lake Michigan, to reach Ensminger Orchards.

Vernon and Maia's house was nothing special. It was just an ordinary one-story, white frame house with no claim to either architectural or historic significance. Any significance the farm had came from the outbuildings. The house was surrounded by well-maintained barns, machine sheds, and storage buildings. The property gave the impression of prosperity, but it looked as if every cent had been plowed back into the orchard business. The house was unimportant in the overall layout.

I might have blamed Vernon for this, but the yard Aunt Nettie and I parked beside didn't look special, either, and that was usually the farmwife's responsibility. There was no fence or flower bed. The shrubs needed trimming, and one lone tree had been planted smack in the middle of the patch of grass that passed for a lawn. The only other trees nearby were peaches and apples planted in the usual neat rows.

Aunt Nettie got out of the van with the pot of ivy she'd bought at the grocery store. I moved close to her and spoke softly. "From the looks of the yard, we're abandoning this poor ivy to a terrible fate."

"It's only a plant, Lee." Aunt Nettie's voice was sharp.

As we walked toward the porch, Vernon opened the door. "Oh, hello," he said awkwardly. "It was nice of you to drop by."

I expected him to step back and invite us in, but he didn't. He just stood there, blocking the door, as we approached. Then he stepped outside and let the storm door close behind him.

That was certainly not hospitable. But it was surprising.

Aunt Nettie smiled sweetly, just as if he'd strewn flowers in our path. "We wanted to tell you and Maia how sorry we are about her uncle."

"She's resting." Vernon looked back into the living room nervously. "I'll tell her you came by."

"It must have been a real shock to her," Aunt Nettie said. "Are there other relatives?"

"Not close." Vernon wasn't budging from in front of that door. "My sister was down from Grand Rapids for a couple of hours."

There was a long pause. I didn't know what to say, and apparently Aunt Nettie didn't either. Finally she moved toward the porch, holding out the ivy plant. "We wanted to bring this."

Vernon looked panicky. To take the plant, he had to either move away from the door, toward Aunt Nettie, or he had to let her come within reaching distance of him. He stepped forward, still holding on to the door handle behind him. Then he moved back, still clutching the handle. Apparently he wasn't able to decide which of the two alternatives to pick. I stared. It was fascinating. I could almost read his mind. He couldn't decide if he should let go of the door, or if he should let Aunt Nettie come close enough to . . . to what? See into the house?

What was eating big, old, reliable, solid Vernon?

Then I heard a tinkling laugh. It was Maia's phony ha-ha, but it didn't come from inside the house. It came from my left. I swung my head in that direction, and Maia herself came around the corner.

"Oh, you've brought a plant," she said. "Aren't you two darlings?"

"We're very sorry about Silas," Aunt Nettie said.

Maia made a strange little sound, someplace between a choke and a giggle. "Uncle Silas and I weren't close," she said. "But I guess I'm the only relative he had."

"That's what Vernon said."

Maia made that strange noise again. "It's funny. My grandfather had three children, but my mother was the only one to marry. Except for Aunt Julia, of course. The one who ran off with Dennis Grundy. Of

course, she was from an earlier marriage. She was a
half sister to my mother and Uncle Silas.

"She never contacted the family after she left. If
she had children, we didn't know anything about it."
She giggled or choked again. "So I was the only child
in my generation. And now I've outlived them all.
I'm the last of the Snows."

Vernon moved, finally, letting go of the storm
door. "I thought you were lying down," he said to
Maia.

Was I imagining the challenge in the way Maia
looked at him? "I thought I'd take a walk," she said.

We obviously weren't going to be asked inside, so
Aunt Nettie began to make motions toward leaving.
She handed the ivy to Maia. "We just wanted you
and Vernon to know that we're thinking of you. And
please call on us if there's anything you need."

I decided I'd better chime in. "Yes, if you need . . .
anything, we're here." I turned toward the van, un-
able to think of anything more to say. I had my hand
on the door handle before I was inspired to make
another comment. "And thanks for letting us visit
the cottage."

Maia didn't say anything, but Vernon spoke.
"Don't mention it."

"It's pretty interesting," I said. "I hadn't realized
it had been in use as recently as it had. And the
orchards behind it—they're beautiful."

Maia did that little giggle business again. "What
do you mean by that?"

"Just what I said. The orchard behind the cottage
is beautiful. It looks well-cared-for and perilous—I
mean, productive! The orchard looks productive."

"Silas was a good fruit man," Vernon said. He
moved close to Maia and put his arm around her
shoulder. "He could be cantankerous, but he was a
hard worker."

Maia giggled, then pressed her fingers against her

lips. Aunt Nettie and I said good-bye, then got in the van and drove away. As fast as we decently could.

"Maia's getting stranger and stranger," I said.

"She acted almost normal last night. Subdued, the way she used to act."

We were silent a moment, then I took a deep breath and prepared to tell Aunt Nettie about Aubrey. I began that way. "About Aubrey . . ."

"That really mystifies me," Aunt Nettie said. "Why anybody would shoot at him. But I don't want to talk about him, Lee."

"But, Aunt Nettie, there's something—"

She smiled and patted my hand. "Now, Lee, don't worry. I'm not going to give him any money. And speaking of money, how did we come out on the special order of chocolate-covered Oreos?"

I tried to report on Aubrey once more before we got back to work, but she cut me off again. And during the hour and a half we spent at work that afternoon, she simply refused to talk to me privately. I was completely balked. I had to face it; Aunt Nettie didn't want me to say anything about Aubrey.

When Tracy came in at four, all excited about her upcoming hair appointment, I had to give up on Aunt Nettie. I promised myself I'd talk to her at home.

Tracy was so excited about her new haircut that she had showed up at TenHuis Chocolade an hour early. Aunt Nettie put her to work wrapping Santas until it was time to go, but I'm not sure if Tracy was a lot of help. She was simply bouncing with excitement.

I was relieved when her mom called. "Lee," she said, "I really appreciate you taking Tracy for a haircut."

"I'm glad to hear that. I wouldn't want to do anything you don't approve of."

"I've been trying to get her to cut that stringy mess

for two years. And since it's ol'dumb mom suggesting it, she has refused. She'd look so much better with a body perm."

A body perm? None of the high school girls had a perm. I could see why Tracy had dodged her mother. "I'm going to leave it up to Angie," I said cautiously. "She's the hair expert. I have a feeling she'll suggest a blunt cut. It may still be straight."

Mrs. Roderick laughed. "As long as it's not too strange a color. That's all I'm worried about."

I was worried about a lot more than that. Tracy was setting her heart on a part in Aubrey's movie—a movie I believed would never be filmed. On the way over to Angie's shop I tried to warn her.

"Tracy, this Mr. Armstrong—don't forget he's a stranger. Just because he claims to be a movie producer—"

"Oh, Lee! You talk just like Mrs. McNutt."

"Mrs. McNutt and I have been around talent shows and beauty pageants, Tracy. We've learned the hard way. A lot of these guys are not for real. They just want to take advantage of pretty girls."

"Pretty girls?" Tracy's voice was awed.

I pressed the point home. "Young, pretty girls like you, Tracy."

She thought a moment, and when she spoke her voice was slightly subdued. "Mr. Armstrong told me never to go to any sort of tryout without my parents." Then she bounced back. "But I still want a new hairdo."

Poor Tracy. She didn't want her dream punctured, but it was going to be.

Angie's skill made Tracy look a lot more grown-up, as well as more attractive. I hung around and put in my two cents' worth while Angie did her makeup. Then Tracy insisted on taking me out to dinner at the Dock Street Pizza Place. She wanted to show off her new look at the main community hangout. Joe was tied up with a city council meeting, so she knew I didn't have a date. It would have been cruel not to go along.

The result was that by the time I got home Aunt Nettie had gone to bed.

It wasn't late, but her door was shut and there was no light under it. I banged around in the kitchen for a while, but Aunt Nettie didn't come out.

I went to bed and read a book. I read quite a long while, actually. It seemed that every time I turned out the light I heard the *thunk* of that rifle bullet hitting Aubrey's SUV.

Once I got off to sleep, I must have slept soundly. Anyway, when Aunt Nettie came to my room, she had to shake me before I was able to wake up.

"Lee. Lee!" Her voice was quiet. "There's somebody outside."

I sat up. Suddenly I felt wide awake. "What going on?"

"I heard somebody on the porch, right outside my window."

I got up and grabbed a robe and slippers. Then I went to the bedroom across the hall. I looked out the window over the porch roof, trying to see if someone was in the yard. I couldn't see anybody, and I couldn't hear anybody.

"Something slid across the porch," Aunt Nettie said. "It sounded like sandpaper. But when I looked out, I couldn't see anything."

"Did you turn on the porch light?"

"Well, no. I guess I didn't really want to see anything. Or I didn't want whoever was out there to see anything." She sighed. "Maybe it was an animal."

"A raccoon doing woodworking?" I looked at my watch. Six a.m. Which in Michigan in October means it was still dark as a piece of Aunt Nettie's bitterest chocolate.

The two of us crept down the stairs and into Aunt

Nettie's bedroom. I peeked through one curtain, and she peeked through another. At first I saw nothing but blackness. But in a moment my eyes grew slightly accustomed to the dark, and I saw something white. It was definitely larger than a bread box. It was about the size of the big packing box my new computer had come in.

"Somebody's put something on the porch," I whispered. "But I don't think anybody is moving around. Let's turn on the light."

Aunt Nettie and I went into the living room, and she flipped the switch beside the front door to turn on the porch light.

Immediately an ungodly noise cut loose.

It was a dog barking.

Chapter 10

Once the light was on, both Aunt Nettie and I recognized the big white object on the front porch. It was a pet crate. And we could hardly mistake the barking.

We spoke in unison. "It's Monte!"

We rushed out the front door. I expected to see Aubrey's SUV sitting in the lane. It wasn't. I ran around the corner of the house and looked in the drive. The porch light was bright enough that I could see there was no SUV. Where was Aubrey? Why was Monte there, but not his master?

Apparently Aunt Nettie felt the same way. "Where's Aubrey?" she said.

I came back to the porch. "There's no sign of him. It's strange. I can't imagine Monte without him."

"There's a note taped to the kennel."

Aunt Nettie pulled it off and read it, frowning. Then she handed it to me. It was printed in block letters on a scrap of notebook paper.

"I'll be back in a day or two," I read. "Please look after Monte."

Monte had stopped howling, but he was looking out the window in his kennel. He seemed anxious. A large plastic garbage bag sat on the floor beside the kennel. When I looked inside, I saw Monte's belongings: food, treats, toys, and another thing that seemed to be important at the moment. His leash.

Shivering in the predawn chill—the temperature was in the midforties and I was wearing a robe and slippers—I took Monte out of the kennel and fastened the leash to his collar. He snuffled happily around the porch and followed eagerly when I stepped down onto the front walk. I allowed him to water the grass a few minutes. Then Aunt Nettie took the leash and led him into the house. I brought in the sack of puppy gear. Monte investigated the living room, and Aunt Nettie and I stared at each other.

Aunt Nettie shook her head. "Where could Aubrey have gone without Monte?"

"And why would he leave the dog with us? We're both at the shop all day. We can't take him there."

"And why did he leave him on the porch, kennel and all? Even if he came in the middle of the night, I'd have expected him to come to the door. We'd better try to call him."

"It's only six a.m."

"He's at the Peach Street B&B. Sarajane will be up fixing breakfast."

"I'll make coffee. I guess it's morning for us, too."

Sarajane Harding is one of Aunt Nettie's brisk, no-nonsense friends. She runs a bed and breakfast inn with four guest rooms, which she handles all by herself. In decor, her B&B simply drips country. Her hat racks are made from garden trellises, the hall is thick with baskets of dried flowers decorated with calico ribbons, the front porch features a watering trough used as a planter, plaster geese march up the stairs, quilts are used as wall hangings. All this contrasts mightily with Sarajane herself, who is a plump sixty-year-old with straight gray hair she apparently cuts with a bowl. She's one of the most efficient business-women I've ever run into.

While I made the coffee and kept an eye on Monte, I eavesdropped on Aunt Nettie's conversation.

"Sarajane? Sorry to bother you. I know you're cooking breakfast. But is Aubrey Armstrong there?"

Aunt Nettie paused. "No, I wouldn't expect him to be down yet. But we thought he must have gone out early."

Another pause. "Would you mind checking his room?"

She listened. "No, I'm sure nothing's wrong. But we woke up to find Monte"—Sarajane apparently broke in, but Aunt Nettie went on quickly—"yes, Monte the dog. He was on my front porch in his crate. And there's a note from Aubrey. He says he's leaving town."

I could hear Sarajane's squawk clearly. "Leaving town!"

"He's coming back! Sarajane! Sarajane!" Aunt Nettie looked at me with consternation. "She dropped the phone."

I laughed. "Well, news that Aubrey is leaving town would certainly get Sarajane to run up and check to see if he's there."

"Oh, dear. I do hope he hasn't done a flit. Hogan was so sure it would be all right."

"Hogan? Chief Jones?"

I wanted to ask more, but Aunt Nettie brushed my question aside. Sarajane was back on the other end of the line.

"His bed hasn't been slept in? Oh, dear. But his things are there?"

She listened again. "The note he left out here said he had to leave Warner Pier for a day or two. But it certainly indicated he intended to come back. I can't imagine him leaving Monte. He really loves that dog."

Sarajane spoke. Aunt Nettie nodded. "Yes. If his clothes and luggage are in the room, it means he intends to come back, Sarajane. But Lee and I don't understand why he left the dog with us." She listened. "All right. I'll wait."

She turned to me. "Sarajane's going to check the parking lot."

"I don't think she'll find Aubrey or his SUV there."

"Neither do I."

I put out the toaster, then looked through Monte's sack until I found his food. "Do you know how often Aubrey feeds him?"

Aunt Nettie shook her head. Then she concentrated on the phone. "Oh? I'm afraid I'm not surprised, Sarajane. But don't worry. I'm sure Aubrey will be back. I'm positive that he wouldn't leave Monte."

She hung up. "Sarajane says she didn't find anything in the guest parking area but a bunch of cigarette butts. Aubrey's SUV is not there."

She tapped her fingers on the telephone. "I guess we'd better tell Hogan about this."

I was surprised. "I don't think we can report someone missing just because he went off and left his dog."

"Oh, but Hogan can put out an all-points bulletin or something for Aubrey. I know he doesn't want to lose track of him."

I didn't even ask Aunt Nettie why the police chief would be interested in Aubrey. All I could think of was Sarajane Harding and the Peach Street B&B. Had Aubrey taken off for good? Was he going to leave Sarajane and other Warner Pier merchants stuck with bills? Had he used stolen or phony credit cards?

I'd been worrying about Aubrey fooling Maia,

Aunt Nettie, and Tracy. I hadn't given a thought to his cheating my fellow Warner Pier merchants.

Now I did, and the thought scared me stiff. If my friends and business associates lost money because I'd fooled around trying to let Aunt Nettie down easily, trying to protect Maggie McNutt, it was going to be humiliating. It could even leave me open to some sort of legal problems, I wasn't sure just what. And it could cost me some friends, and I need all of those I can get.

Then Monte came into the kitchen, snuffling around as he investigated his surroundings.

Could Aubrey really have abandoned Monte? It was hard to believe he'd leave the pup with Aunt Nettie and me. We had no fence, and we couldn't take him to TenHuis Chocolade for the day.

I could only hope that Chief Hogan Jones would have some suggestion that would lead to finding Aubrey.

I knelt down and scratched Monte under the chin. This made him flop over onto his back for a tummy rub. I complied.

"Monte," I said. "I wish you'd tell us just where your master has gone. I'm not sure I know how to take care of you."

In the garbage bag I found a red blanket covered with Monte's silky brown hair, and I spread it out in the corner of the dining room. Monte sniffed at it, turned around three times in the traditional manner of dogs, then lay down for a snooze while Aunt Nettie and I sat down at the breakfast table. It was then I realized that, for the first time since I'd talked to Maggie McNutt about Aubrey nearly twenty-four hours earlier, I now had a chance to tell Aunt Nettie what I'd learned about him. I sighed.

"Aunt Nettie, I'm afraid I've got some bad news for you," I said. Then I detailed my fruitless Internet search. "Unless I'm looking for Aubrey under entirely the wrong name, I just don't see how he can be a real movie producer," I said.

Aunt Nettie smiled. "Oh, I know that, Lee."

"You do? Then why—"

"Why did I encourage his attentions? Well, there is a reason, but it's not my secret. But don't worry about my giving him any money."

"I know you're smarter than *that*."

Aunt Nettie spread peach preserves on her toast. "It's refreshing for an old woman—"

"You're not old," I said.

Aunt Nettie ignored me. "—for an old woman to feel that she can still be attractive to a man. And Aubrey is—I guess the word is 'likeable,' Lee. I enjoy being with him, even when I'm reminding myself that every word he says is a lie. He's good company."

"I'll admit that. I'm just afraid you're going to get your feelings hurt."

"I might. But even if I do, Aubrey's been fun. He's jogged me out of my rut."

I made a few more attempts to get Aunt Nettie to tell me what had inspired her to court attention from Aubrey if she knew he was moving under false pretenses, but she didn't answer. So I dropped it. But I felt deeply relieved that she hadn't been fooled by him.

We ended our breakfast conversation by talking about Monte and why we were stuck with him. Neither of us had any fresh ideas.

As she left the table, Aunt Nettie shook her head. "I guess I'll take a shower. We've still got to get the shop open."

"I'll do the dishes and try to think of somebody who can babysit Monte," I said. "I guess some people leave dogs in those portable kennels all day, but I don't think Monte's used to that."

"I guess we should give him some breakfast." Aunt Nettie sounded doubtful. "I wouldn't know how much or how to fix it."

I had a sudden thought. "You know who has always had dogs? Lindy and Tony Herrera. I'll give Lindy a ring and ask her about feeding a half-grown pup."

My idea turned out to be an inspiration. Lindy first told me a pup like Monte would normally be fed morning and night, and she described how to prepare the food I'd found among his belongings. Then she actually offered to let us leave Monte in her fenced backyard for the day.

"What will Pinto say?" I asked cautiously. Pinto is Lindy's ancient mixed-breed dog. The three Herrera kids claim she's named "Pinto" because she's marked with big black and white spots like a pinto pony. She's also nearly as big as a pinto pony. Tony Herrera says she's named for the bean, for reasons Lindy won't let him explain. But Pinto rules Tony and Lindy's backyard with an iron paw.

"Pinto's usually good with pups," Lindy said. "Since all the kids figured out where babies come from we've put her out of the puppy business. But she still has some maternal instinct. I'll be home today. I can keep an eye out."

I'd hung up before I remembered that Lindy had promised to tell me some gossip. I made a mental note to ask about it when I dropped Monte off.

It was nearly nine o'clock when I led Monte out to my van and said, "Kennel," speaking firmly, as Aubrey had. The pup jumped right into his crate, and I felt a thrill of accomplishment. I remembered to give him a dog treat before I shut the door.

I had decided to cart the kennel along, for one thing, because Monte was used to being in it while riding in a car. And for another, Lindy might want to use it if the two dogs had to be separated. I also

brought Monte's blanket, treats, food, and some of
his toys. When I arrived at Lindy's she looked a bit
amazed at all the paraphernalia.

"I promise I'll take it all away this afternoon," I
said. "But I don't know what you'll need. I can leave
the kennel in the van."

Lindy knelt down and gave Monte a good tummy
scratch. "If he and Pinto don't get along, I might use
the kennel."

I unloaded the van, then went to the backyard with
Lindy to watch as Pinto and Monte got acquainted.
Lindy's prediction seemed to be right. Monte frisked
around, yapping and barking at the older dog. Pinto
took it for a few minutes, then gave one deep woof
and put Monte in his place. She lay down regally and
watched the pup explore her domain. Since Lindy's
backyard had a hedge as well as a fence all around
it, up the sides and along the alley, Monte had plenty
of nooks and crannies to explore.

Lindy and I sat on the back step. "What did you
call me about yesterday?" I asked. "I called back, but
I missed you."

"I wondered if you wanted to buy a house."

"Oh, Lindy, has your house deal fallen through?"

"It looks like it. Wouldn't you and Joe be interested? Joe could handle a fixer-upper."

"Joe and I—things are too unsettled between us
for us to be buying a house, Lindy. But I thought
Ken and Maggie were interested in it."

"We thought we had a deal. But Ken called yesterday. He says they might leave at the end of the year."

"Leave! Did he say why?"

"No. In fact, he was extremely evasive. But we
need to find another buyer."

"I hope you don't lose the Vandermeer house."

"So do I. But we can't sign on that until we sell
this one."

I went to work then, but the conversation had left me feeling low. Ken and Maggie were thinking of leaving Warner Pier? I guess we'd all known that a drama teacher as talented as Maggie would eventually get the call to a bigger school, but they'd seemed happy in Warner Pier. Could Aubrey Andrews Armstrong be the problem? Was Maggie so sure he'd tell about her scandalous past that she was already assuming she wouldn't get another contract?

I spoke aloud. "If Aubrey comes back alive, I'll kill him."

Yes, it was imperative that we find Aubrey. I was glad to discover that Aunt Nettie was already doing something about this when I got to TenHuis Chocolade. She and Chief Hogan Jones were conferring in the break room.

"I've got the sheriff talking to every gas station in the county, and the state police checking up and down the interstate," Hogan said. "If Armstrong used a credit card, we should be able to figure which way he went."

"But he could have gotten beyond Chicago on less than a tank of gas," I said. "Checking the stations looks like a long shot. Besides, what's to stop him from going anywhere he wants to go? He's not wanted for anything, is he?"

Hogan didn't answer. Instead, Aunt Nettie spoke. "I simply can't believe Aubrey took it on the lam. I mean, he might run away, but he wouldn't leave Monte."

Hogan nodded. "That would look like a definite break in the pattern."

I was mystified. "What pattern?"

Hogan hung his head and kicked a chair, but before he could answer the phone rang. I answered on the break room extension. "TenHuis Chocolade."

"Hello, Lee." The voice was unmistakable.

"Hi, Maia. What can I do for you?"

"I was looking for Aubrey. I don't suppose you or Nettie knows where he is."

"No. In fact, we're trying to find him." I quickly sketched our discovery of Monte on the front porch and told her we were completely mystified about where he had gone and why he'd left the dog with us. "Lindy Herrera is dog-sitting today," I said.

"Oh, Lindy has a big yard. That's a good place for Monte."

"Yes, we appreciated Lindy's offer. But if you hear from Aubrey, or if you track him down, we'd sure like to know what's going on."

Chief Jones was nearly out the back door when I hung up. "Wait!" I said. "Have you found out anything about that shot?"

"The one that nearly hit Armstrong? Nope."

"Did you figure out where it came from?"

"Not exactly. The sheriff and I took Aubrey's SUV out there and parked it at what Joe said was the same spot. We tried to figure the angle. All we could tell was that it came from someplace off to the north and up high."

"Up high? Like a tree?"

"Or the second story of a house. Or a telephone pole."

"Is there a two-story house or a telephone pole in the right spot?"

"Hard to say." That was the chief's final word, and I realized it could mean either "I don't know" or "I don't want to tell you." Either way, I didn't find out anything.

Warner Pier was up to its small-town tricks that day. The phone nearly rang off the wall with people wanting to know about Aubrey and Monte. At first I was amazed at how fast word had gotten around, but I soon traced the path the information had followed.

Sarajane had apparently told the laundry service deliveryman, because we heard from several more B&Bs. Lindy had told her mother, who told her dad, who's an electrician, and he happened to be working at the Superette that morning. And once the news that Aubrey had left Monte on our porch and gone on some mysterious trip hit the druggist at the Superette's pharmacy, Greg Gossip—I mean, Glossop—we might as well have sent a truck with a loudspeaker blaring the news up and down the streets.

I was kept busy answering the phone and telling people we had no reason to believe that Aubrey wouldn't come back to get Monte. I also assured them that I hadn't heard that the state detectives were unusually interested in Aubrey as a suspect in the killing of Silas Snow. A few of the more curious even came into the shop to ask about it. I gave those a hard sell and managed to get some of them to buy a few chocolates.

The morning had been quite hectic, and I wasn't pleased when, about twelve thirty, the phone rang yet again. It was an effort to make my voice cheerful when I answered. "TenHuis Chocolade."

"Lee! It's Lindy! You'd better get out here. This pup's sick! The dog got hold of some chocolate!"

CHOCOLATE CHAT

GOOD FOR WHAT AILS YOU

Chocolate may well help when you have tummy trouble. Intestinal upsets or even a round of antibiotics can upset the balance of lactase enzymes and bacteria needed to digest milk. This produces a form of lactose intolerance. In one study, researchers at the University of Rhode Island discovered that drinking a cup of milk to which 1½ teaspoons of cocoa had been added helped half of their subjects—all of them lactose intolerant—deal with their problem. (In some people, sadly, chocolate can relax the esophageal sphincter muscle and allow stomach acid to shoot up into the esophagus, resulting in heartburn.)

Chocolate is a good source of minerals, since it contains magnesium, potassium, chromium, and iron, and is commonly used as a sort of home remedy for the blues. This is not just self-indulgence. Chocolate actually contains mood-lifting chemicals such as caffeine and theobromine. Mixed with sugar and fat, it produces chemicals that promote euphoria and calm. Some women use chocolate to fight mild forms of PMS.

Lastly, in animal experiments, some test subjects reduced their intake of alcohol when they were offered a chocolate drink as an alternative. Chocolate martini, anyone?

Chapter 11

I squealed to a stop in Lindy's drive, ran around the house, and went in the back gate. Lindy was sitting on the back step, petting Monte. He hadn't rolled over to ask for a tummy rub.

As I watched, he got up and sprinkled the grass. Then he gagged once or twice.

"I called the vet," Lindy said. "He said it doesn't sound as if he got enough to be fatal, but he said maybe we'd better take him in. After all, Monte's a valuable dog."

"What about Pinto? She's awfully valuable to your kids."

"She ate chocolate, too, but she's a bigger dog. It would take more to hurt her."

"How do you know the dogs ate chocolate?"

Lindy held up a plastic sack. In it were several of the silvery paper squares from baking chocolate, the same stuff I buy at the Superette to make brownies. All of them were torn and chewed. There were also a couple of the squares themselves, still wrapped.

"Baking chocolate?" I was amazed. "I'd been

thinking some kid walked by and tossed the dogs a bite of his candy bar. That looks as if somebody threw a whole package into the yard."

"That's what I think, too. This was no accident. Someone did it deliberately."

"Did you see anybody?"

"No, the dogs seemed to be getting along all right, so I was in the house, trying to get the washing done. I think whoever tossed the chocolate in came up the back alley, anyway. The hedge would have kept me from seeing anybody."

Lindy called her mother and asked her to be there when the kids got home from school. She said she'd already called Tony to tell him what had happened. Then we loaded both dogs into my van and drove the thirty minutes to Holland, where the nearest veterinarian—the one Lindy took Pinto to—was located. The vet's assistant took both dogs right into the examining rooms and directed Lindy and me to the waiting area.

Lindy had gone to the ladies' room when Chief Jones came in.

"What are you doing here?" I said.

"Tony Herrera called and said his dog had been poisoned. That's a crime. I thought the Warner Pier Police Department ought to look into it. The state police are a little too high-toned to investigate a dog poisoning."

"Why would you think the state police might consider being involved?"

"Ever since Silas Snow was killed, it seems as if all sorts of things are happening to animals and people who were hooked up with Aubrey Andrews Armstrong."

I clutched his arm. "Nothing's happened to Aunt Nettie?"

"What could happen to her?"

"I don't know. You just frightened me."

"No, Nettie's all right. Which is more than I can say for Silas. And Vernon says Mae Ensminger is sick. Of course, I ought to bawl out both you and Nettie for making a lot of tracks in your driveway before she called to tell me Monte had been dumped off on your porch."

"We had to go to work. Why shouldn't we have left tracks in the driveway?"

"If I'd seen the drive before you drove out, it might have helped me figure out how the dog got onto your front porch."

"Is there any question about that? Aubrey obviously drove up, stopped in the drive, got the kennel out of his SUV, and put it on our porch."

"Nettie says she didn't hear a car stop."

"I didn't ask her about that. She said she heard somebody on the porch, and I assumed that a car had driven up."

Hogan shook his head. "When I quizzed her about the details, I realized that wasn't the way it happened. All she heard was something—the kennel, I guess—sliding across the porch. No, apparently somebody walked up to the house from Lake Shore Drive. The guy had to carry the kennel and the dog and that sack of stuff. It must have taken at least two trips."

"I guess Aubrey didn't want to wake us up."

"Maybe so. But I wonder where Aubrey would have gotten a wheelbarrow."

"A wheelbarrow? He used a wheelbarrow?"

"Yep. I managed to find bits and pieces of the tracks of a wheelbarrow coming up your lane from Lake Shore Drive. You can see the single track of the wheel, and I even found the places where the back supports rested on the ground not far from the porch."

"But that's an awfully complicated way to put a kennel with a dog on a front porch. Driving up would be much easier. Why didn't he do that?"

"The obvious reason is that he definitely did not want Nettie to wake up and catch him doing it."

"I know she would have told him we couldn't keep the dog, but still . . . I don't understand. Why would Aubrey be *that* anxious not to be seen? And, like you say, where would he get a wheelbarrow?"

Hogan sat back and looked at me, obviously inviting me to think it over. Gradually the light dawned.

"Hogan," I said. "Are you trying to tell me Aubrey didn't drop Monte on our porch? Somebody else did?"

"I can't be sure just what happened, Lee. But it sure seems possible."

"Have you asked Mae about Aubrey? He came to Warner Pier to see her. It seems as if he wouldn't leave without saying good-bye."

"I talked to Vernon. He said he doesn't know anything about Aubrey. And he says Mae is sick in bed. I didn't get to talk to her."

"I admit Mae acted pretty strange when I saw her yesterday. Maybe she *is* sick. But I don't know what that would have to do with Aubrey taking off."

"If he took off."

I finally saw what Hogan was getting at. "You think something's happened to him."

"I don't know, Lee. But you, Joe, and Nettie all swear somebody shot at him yesterday. And nobody's seen him since late last night. Now it seems somebody has it in for his dog. That's what I'd call suspicious."

Lindy came back then, and Chief Jones took the particulars of when she'd found the sick dogs. She handed over the uneaten chocolate and its silver wrappers. Then the chief went away, leaving my head whirling.

Maybe Aubrey hadn't simply left town. Maybe he was missing. Kidnapped? Killed?

But in my scenario, based on Aubrey's status as the invisible movie producer and on Maggie's description of him as a blackmailer, Aubrey was supposed to be the crook. He should be the leading suspect in the killing of Silas Snow, for example. But now it seemed Aubrey might have become a victim.

How was Aunt Nettie going to react to this?

And what was Maia up to? She had called me earlier, trying to find Aubrey, but now Vernon said she couldn't talk to Chief Jones. I felt sure she was simply hiding behind Vernon. I felt impatient with her; she'd attracted Aubrey to Warner Pier with her silly novel and had drawn all of us into this mess. Now she had gone to bed with a headache. Darn her anyway, I thought. First she dragged Vernon around, treating him like a flunky, then she made him cover for her.

Before I had a chance to tell Lindy what I'd learned about Aubrey, the vet came out and told us we could take Pinto home. I was relieved when he asked to keep Monte overnight. At least the pup was safe there. Maybe Aubrey would even show up to pay the bill.

Lindy loaded Pinto into the van, and we drove back to Warner Pier. I started to tell Lindy what the chief had said, but Pinto headed off any confidences by upchucking on the floor of the backseat, as the vet had said she might, and Lindy became so upset over a mess in someone else's vehicle that I gave up trying to talk to her.

I had to wait around at Lindy's while she insisted on cleaning up Pinto's mess and spraying the van with air freshener. By the time I got away I'd nearly forgotten everything but sick dogs.

I remembered my other concerns, however, when I came to the Peach Street stoplight. I was on the flashing-red side and had to come to a stop and wait for a farm truck to cross on the yellow. That farm truck had ENSMINGER'S ORCHARDS lettered on the door and was driven by Vernon. And it was not headed toward his house. Vernon was not on the way home.

I watched Vernon go on down the street. He parked in front of the hardware store, got out of his truck, and went inside.

If Vernon was at the hardware store, then Maia was probably alone at the farm, and maybe I'd be able to talk to her. I simply had to find out if she knew where Aubrey could be. If nothing else, I couldn't be responsible for Monte if someone was trying to harm him.

I abruptly turned left and headed out of town.

Maia and Vernon's place once again impressed me with the attention that had been paid to the outbuildings, in contrast to the slightly neglected look of the house. I parked in front and walked up on the porch, being careful to make noise. It's not polite to sneak up on anybody who lives out in the country.

I had knocked three times and had nearly given up when I heard a horn honk behind me. I whirled to see a sedan turning into the road. The car was a sedate tan, but it was being driven as if it were a bright red, souped-up sports model. I saw Maia's mop of black hair behind the wheel.

She skidded to a stop on the gravel drive, throwing up a cloud of dust, then jumped out of the car. "Lee! Have you found Aubrey?"

Maia looked awful. Her hair was matted, her makeup was streaked. She wore her usual black pants and shirt, but they looked as if she'd slept in them. She'd left off her clunky jewelry, and instead of her usual black ballet-type slippers, she wore tennis shoes.

She trotted up onto the porch. "Where is he? I must find him!"

"I haven't heard from Aubrey," I said. "I came here hoping you knew something."

"Drat the man! A plague on him!"

A plague on him? Hmmm. "I wondered if he gave you any kind of hint as to where he was going."

"Come in, come in!" Maia pushed past me, opened the unlocked door, and led me inside a living room that was as bedraggled as the outside of the house. She staggered over to a tired-looking plaid couch and sat down. "I went over to the Peach Street B&B to see if he was there."

"Sarajane told Aunt Nettie it looked as if he hadn't come in last night. You know he left Monte with Aunt Nettie and me."

"I heard that—from somebody. Was it you?" Maia's eyes closed. "But you palmed him off on Lindy Herrera."

"Just for the day, Maia. Lindy was keeping him while Aunt Nettie and I were at work. But somebody fed the poor thing chocolate."

Maia licked her lips and gave a giggle. "Chocolate sounds good."

"It's good for people. But it's poison to dogs."

"I know." Her eyes took on a crafty look. "Is Monte dead?"

"Monte? No. The vet says he'll be all right. But I need to tell Aubrey what's happened to him. Are you sure he didn't give you any idea of where he was going? When did you last talk to him?"

Maia got up and paced around the living room. "I haven't seen him or talked to him since Tuesday night, since we all went to dinner at the Warner River Lodge." Her voice took on a singsong quality. "I came home about four. I took a long, soaking bath. I lay down and rested for half an hour. I got dressed. Aubrey and Nettie came around seven, and we went out to dinner. Afterward, they dropped us off. They didn't come in. Vernon and I went straight to bed. Vernon was here all the time."

It was a rather peculiar answer, but none of Maia's comments were making too much sense. I tried a new tack. "Maia, when did you first hear from Aubrey?"

"First?"

"Yes. When did he first call about buying the movie rights to your book? Last week? Last month?"

"Sometime." Maia ran her fingers through her hair, or at least she tried. They got stuck in some of the tangles, and she gave up and simply pulled the fingers loose. "Aubrey called the day before he showed up," she said. "That was Monday. He drove in Tuesday morning. Why does it matter?"

"If I could track down some of his associates, maybe they know how to find him. He must have a secretary." Or he would if he were a genuine movie producer. I left that unspoken.

Maia puffed herself up like a bird on a cold morning. "If he has a secretary, it isn't I," she said.

"I know that."

"Everybody keeps asking me about Aubrey, just as if I was his secretary."

"Everybody?"

Maia made another try at tossing her matted hair. "People."

She flopped back onto the couch. Her getting up and sitting down and pacing back and forth was beginning to make me as nervous as it apparently made her. I decided I was wasting my time. One more question. "Did Aubrey give you an address for his California offices?"

"No!" Maia laughed, but she didn't sound pleased. "Aubrey's a man of mystery. I'm beginning to realize that."

"Thanks for letting me ask you all these questions,

Maia. I'll go now." I turned toward the door. But before I could open it I heard footsteps outside. They were approaching swiftly. I opened the door and saw Vernon trotting up the steps.

His face was screwed up. With anger? That wouldn't have surprised me. But when he spoke his voice didn't sound angry. I wasn't sure what emotion it had, but it didn't seem to be anger.

"What are you doing here?"

"I wanted to talk to Maia, but I shouldn't have bothered her."

Vernon came in the front door. "Maia! Where did you go?"

"Just over to the Peach Street B&B, Vernon." There was an undertone of guilt in Maia's voice.

"You should have taken your medicine." Vernon shifted his stare from Maia to me. "Why did you want to talk to her?"

"I'm still trying to find some black gown on Aubrey." Vernon's jaw dropped, and I felt like an idiot. "Background! I mean, I'm trying to find some background about Aubrey."

I went on quickly, determined to change the subject to one that wouldn't make me feel nervous. "By the way, Vernon, I grew up in farming and ranching country, you know, and I want to tell you how impressive your layout is."

"My layout?"

"Ensminger's Orchards. The barns and storage buildings just sparkle. The equipment looks great. The orchards are neat as a pin. How much help do you have?"

I asked a few more questions. This seemed to thaw Vernon. He began to look calm, then even to show a bit of enthusiasm. I tried another question. "Did you grow up on a fruit fly? I mean, farm! Did you grow up on a fruit farm?"

"No, I didn't know a thing about farming before Mae and I got married. Everything I know about orchards I learned from Silas."

"Then his death must have been a double shock to you, Vernon."

He nodded. But he didn't say anything.

I tried to look understanding. "I know. The police inquiry and everything. It's dreadful."

Vernon sighed. "Mae and I have been over it and over it. We came home about four. Mae took a bath, then laid down for a while. I worked on my crop report. Then I took a shower. We got dressed and went out to dinner. Aubrey and Nettie picked us up at seven."

Vernon was answering a question I hadn't asked. And we seemed to be covering old territory. I headed for the door. "I'm sorry I bothered you all. Maia needs to get some rest."

"She will. I'll see to that."

I paused in the doorway and asked one more question.

"As you can tell, I'm not familiar with fruit growing. There's one piece of equipment that's always stumped me. The three-legged ladder. Why is it better than a regular ladder?"

Maia giggled. I stared at her, but Vernon ignored her. "It's really just a stepladder," he said. "It rests against the branches. But the leg keeps the weight of the ladder and the picker off the tree. Besides, the leg can snake through the branches and keep the ladder steady."

Maia shook her tousled head. "Forget the ladder," she said. "I don't want to talk about any ladder."

Vernon and I stared at her. She giggled vigorously. "I'm just a secretary. Maybe an answering machine."

She was repeating the comment she'd made a few minutes earlier. I decided to try for information.

"You mean being asked to take messages for Aubrey? Who asked you to do that?"

"That newspaper guy."

"Chuck O'Riley? What did he want?"

"Nosy. Jus' nosy."

Vernon's face looked as if he'd been kicked. It reminded me that he had sobbed at the funeral home. When I said good-bye he mumbled an answer. Then he walked out on the porch and watched until I drove off.

I certainly hadn't gotten any real information from Maia. But she had sparked an idea. The more I thought about it, the more I liked it.

As soon as I got to my desk I called Chuck O'Riley.

Chapter 12

Calling Chuck may have been my intent, but life intervened. My working life that is. I'd been gone most of the afternoon, but TenHuis Chocolade had been rocking along. Before I could call anybody I had to go through a pile of messages Aunt Nettie had taken while I'd been gone. Most of them could wait, but I had to call the bank, then do an invoice for five pounds of crème de menthe bonbons, which would adorn the pillows of the new Gray Gables Conference Center. Aunt Nettie had already boxed them up. I'd deliver them on my way home.

When I finally called Chuck, he sounded harassed. "You barely caught me," he said. "This is supposed to be my day off."

"I guess I knew that, Chuck. Since the *Gazette* came out today. But I'll trade you a half pound of Ten-Huis's best for the answer to a question."

"What's the question?"

"Have you looked into the background of Aubrey Andrews Armstrong?"

There was a long silence. Chuck cleared his throat. Then he spoke. "Why do you ask?"

"I tried to look him up on the Internet, just out of curiosity. And I couldn't find him there. I wondered if you had better sources."

"I hadn't tried to find out anything about him until he disappeared. I couldn't find out anything on the Internet either. So I called the Michigan Film Office."

"I e-mailed them. The director was out of town."

"She still is, but someone should call me back pretty quick."

"Did Aubrey give you a business card? Or anything in writing?"

"No. Lee, why do you want to know this?"

"I need to find Aubrey. I guess you've heard that he dumped his dog on Aunt Nettie and me."

"I also heard the dog was poisoned. I wasn't going to do the story today, since I can't get it in the paper until next week, but what's the deal on that? A dog poisoner would be worth a story."

That was something I didn't mind talking about. I told Chuck all about it. When I'd finished, he spoke. "What are you going to do about the dog when he's well?"

"I hope Aubrey will be back by then."

"Chief Jones seems to think something has happened to the guy. What do you think?"

"I haven't the slightest idea. I hope Aubrey has taken off on some sort of trip. And I also hope he'll be back soon to take responsibility for Monte. That's why I was asking if you had some contact information for him."

"I interviewed him, of course. Anything I learned about him is in today's *Gazette*, Lee."

I began to wonder if the *Gazette* had information on other topics. "How complete are your files, Chuck?"

"We've got all the back issues. Either bound or on microfilm."

"How about files on people?"

"You mean, like Lee McKinney is named business manager of TenHuis Chocolade? Or Joe Woodyard takes job as city attorney? Yeah, we've got stuff like that."

"Do you let the public look at it?"

"Sure. You're welcome to come by the office and look at our files. But not today. Tomorrow morning. Okay?"

I could hardly ask Chuck to stick around on his day off just to satisfy my curiosity. I agreed to wait until morning. Then I hung up and gave myself a pep talk about getting my own work done. That resolve lasted about ten minutes, until Dolly Jolly appeared in the door of my office.

Her voice boomed. "Lee! I wanted to talk to you before I left!"

I tried not to grimace as I looked up. After all, I was supposed to be running the paycheck and health insurance side of TenHuis Chocolade. I couldn't refuse to speak to employees.

"What can I do for you, Dolly?"

Dolly lowered her voice to a low roar. "It's sort of private."

Oh, gosh. It was something important. Or personal. Did she need time off? Was she sick? I hoped she hadn't already decided she hated the chocolate business; Aunt Nettie was really pleased at how quickly Dolly was catching on.

My uneasiness grew when Dolly came in and closed the door, isolating the two of us in the glass cubicle. I waved her to a chair. "This looks serious, Dolly."

"It's serious to me," she said. Dolly's freckled face was getting red. She didn't go on immediately, but took several deep breaths before she spoke again.

"This Mae Ensminger," she said. "Do you think she's mentally ill?"

I was astonished. Why on earth would Dolly ask such a question? And why would she ask me? Anyway, the answer popped out.

"How the heck would I know?"

Then I felt terrible, because Dolly looked more miserable than ever. She had obviously wanted something more than a smart-aleck answer.

"You've been around her a lot," she said. "You're a smart person. I'm just asking you for your opinion, not for a diagnosis."

"Why do you care?"

Dolly looked down and did something I'd never seen her do before. She mumbled. "I guess I don't really have a good excuse," she said. "I just wondered if insanity runs in her family. Her uncle was kind of odd. And if her real grandfather was like the one in the book . . ."

This was certainly the strangest conversation I'd had in a long time. But it was very serious to Dolly. I didn't want to give her a brush-off, but I didn't know what to answer.

"Dolly, I never heard that any of them were hospitalized for mental problems," I said. "You could ask Aunt Nettie. Or Hazel. They're the natives here."

"I thought I could ask you, and you wouldn't tell anybody I wanted to know."

"I won't mention it if you don't want me to."

"I just wanted your opinion."

Dolly was still keeping her voice very low, an action that forced her to concentrate. She was naturally a loud person, and speaking in a low voice was hard for her. So I knew this was very serious to her. I tried to give her an intelligent assessment of the Snow clan.

"As for Silas," I said, "Judging by the one time I saw him and by what Vernon said about him, I think he was old-fashioned and cantankerous. But that's a long way from being mentally ill. When it comes to Maia—or Mae—I don't understand what's going on at all. But I think that having that book published went to her head. It certainly changed her personality."

"You think she was okay before this book deal came up?"

"She certainly became a different person. Mae was always colorless. She struck me as really dull. Now . . . it's as if she's working to be a caricature of a novelist."

I had an inspiration. "Listen, Dolly, tomorrow morning I'm going to the *Gazette* office to look up some information. Maybe they have some files on Silas. I'm sure they'll have some on Maia. I'll see what I can find out there."

"I'd appreciate it."

Dolly stood up and moved toward the door. I allowed myself to think that our interview was over.

Then she turned around again. "It's just hard to figure how Maia could get so excited over a vanity book."

After dropping that bombshell, she opened the door and left the office.

I had to take a minute to absorb what she'd said. Then I was out the door after her. "Wait a minute, Dolly! Come back in here."

She came. This time I was the one who closed the door and dropped my voice.

"A 'vanity book'? Are you saying Maia *paid* to get her book published?"

"She must have, Lee."

"How do you know?"

"I wrote a regional cookbook, remember? I talked to every publisher in Michigan—and you'd be surprised at how many there are. That particular publisher told me they do only 'author participation' books. I would have had to come up with around five thousand dollars, then do all my own promotion and distribution. I certainly wasn't interested in that. Not when I got a reputable regional press interested in my book. They didn't pay a lot, but it didn't *cost* me money to get it published. And they do the publicity and distribution. I don't have to create my own press kit and ship my own books."

"Then I could write something—*The ABCs of Office Management*, maybe—and they'd publish it?"

"For a price. They'd print any number you wanted. Then they'd send all the books to you, and you'd sell them. Or store them in your garage."

"Which would be a likely fate for any book I'd write."

"When I heard they were publishing Maia's book, I didn't want to say too much about it," Dolly said. "Maia seemed so proud of her book. I figured she didn't know the difference between vanity publishing and regular publishing. I have no reason to embarrass her."

Dolly left, and I sat at my desk mulling over what Dolly had told me. It made Maia's behavior look really peculiar. There's absolutely nothing wrong with paying to publish a book, I told myself. If you wanted to see your family history or all your grandmother's recipes in print, fine. If Maia's life wasn't going to be complete until *Love Leads the Way* was in print, paying to publish it was worth the money. But why was she acting as if the book's publication were the literary event of the year?

I was aroused from my mulling when the telephone rang. It was Joe. "How about dinner?"

I looked at the work piled up on my desk and sighed. "I'd have to eat in a hurry. I was gone most of the afternoon."

"Taking care of Monte?"

"Among other things. I'm going to have to work

at least a couple of hours. I guess I'd better grab a sandwich and stick to my desk."

"Maybe both of us could do that, then I'll come by your office about nine. If you're still hungry we'll get a bite. If not—well, I'd like to see you."

We left it at that. I hoped Joe wasn't planning some sort of serious discussion of our future. I hadn't had time to figure out where I stood on that.

So I planned to snag a snack from the break room and work on through. But again, someone else changed my plans. This time it was Aunt Nettie.

She came up to my office with a large box in her hands. "Here are the crème de menthe bonbons."

I realized she was holding the five-pound box of crème de menthe bonbons Gray Gables had ordered. "Oh," I said, "I forgot those. I was planning to work late."

"I guess I can take them." Aunt Nettie looked really tired. She had taken the news about Aubrey without flinching, but she'd had a long day. I knew she was dying to get home and get her shoes off.

"Oh, no. I can take them," I said. "No problem."

I told her I was planning to grab a sandwich sometime, so I'd drop off the bonbons when I went out. Then I'd go back to work until Joe picked me up around nine o'clock. She approved and left for home. I closed out the computer, put on my lightweight khaki jacket, and picked up the box of bonbons.

Gray Gables is a historic estate. The High Victorian home on the property was built in the 1890s by a former ambassador and is still owned by his descendants. And like many modern-day people who inherited these snazzy estates, the current owners were having trouble financing the place. Between the taxes for waterfront property in Warner Pier and the staff required to keep up the house and the grounds, the current owners had found themselves in a tight place financially.

So that summer they'd turned the property into a conference center. They took groups of at least twelve and charged a stiff rate. The food, or so I'd heard, was superb. And every night the beds were turned down and a TenHuis crème de menthe bonbon was placed on each pillow.

Usually the owner-operator picked the bonbons up, but today she'd requested that we bring them to her. Five pounds of bonbons was an order well worth driving two miles to deliver. I might even have told myself that a short drive would clear my head, except that I'd already driven all over western Michigan that afternoon, and I had grown more confused than ever.

But the weather had changed a little during the hour and a half I'd been indoors. The wind had switched to the west and had grown stronger. The fall leaves were flying down the street as the wind whipped them off the trees. It wasn't much colder yet, but the change in wind direction meant the temperature was likely to drop into the thirties that night.

Anyway, I put the bonbons on the floor of the van's front seat—I didn't want to take a chance of them sliding off the seat if I should come to a sudden stop—then I drove across the Orchard Street Bridge. The river approaches the lake from the southeast, then makes a sharp right just as it comes to Warner Pier. From there it flows due west into Lake Michigan. Once the road crosses the Orchard Street Bridge, a right hand turn puts you on Lake Shore Drive, curving around along the lake and leading to houses, including the one Aunt Nettie and I shared. To reach Gray Gables I turned left onto Inland Road, which roughly follows the river. I mention all this because it turned out to be important.

The late afternoon sunlight was slanting through the trees, turning the woods to red, gold, orange, rust, purple, and all the glorious colors of fall. October is beautiful everywhere in the northern hemisphere, I guess, but sometimes it seemed as if western Michigan got more than its share of the goodies. I was quite annoyed to see the wind whipping the leaves around, tearing them off prematurely. I want the leaves to stay colorful as long as possible.

For the most part, however, the woods were still thick. That gave me a few qualms, but I reminded myself to look at the beautiful color, not think about how the trees blocked the view of the horizon.

My feelings about trees are typical of people born and raised on the plains, I guess. On the one hand we value trees highly. In my hometown, for example, a building lot with trees costs more than one without, and in plains cities architects design buildings with an eye to saving mature trees. But for us true plains natives, thick woods are scary, just as open plains are scary to people raised in the woods. Aunt Nettie says she felt "exposed" when she visited my North Texas hometown. There was nothing to hide behind. But I feel spooked when I'm in thick woods; something could be hiding behind those trees.

I felt safe in the van, however, and I poked along, enjoying the lovely colors.

There are lots of houses along Inland Road, but they are farther apart as you get near to Gray Gables. In fact, there were no houses for about a half mile before the road came to the estate, and Inland Road dead-ends at its gate. I felt sure the gate would be open, since the conference center was expecting guests, as well as me.

So I was surprised when I saw the wrought iron gate was closed. I stopped, ready to honk for admittance.

As I did, two things happened, suddenly and almost simultaneously.

First, the van grew hard to steer and pulled to the right.

Before I could say, "Rats! I've got a flat," the second thing happened.

The entire windshield became checked, turning magically into opaque glass.

The sound of the shot didn't register in my tiny brain until a moment later.

Chapter 13

In real time it may have been only a split second until I reacted, but at the moment it seemed as if I spent an hour sitting there, staring stupidly at that checkered windshield, not moving, just trying to figure out what had made the appearance of the glass change so magically.

That shattered windshield probably saved my life. I would have been a perfect target if the rifleman could have seen me clearly. The checkered windshield must have made me hard to hit.

Anyway, I heard the second shot as I was diving for the floor. Since the van has captain's chairs, the quickest way to get to the floor was to drop between the seats. I somehow wound up in an L shape, with my head and torso on the floor of the backseat and my legs and feet between the front seats.

At first, driving off didn't seem like a viable option. The van's motor was still running, true, but I couldn't see out the front window at all, and I had a flat. I wouldn't be able to drive off very fast.

When the third shot hit, however, driving off began to seem like the smartest way to go.

I pulled my legs into the backseat—not the most graceful trick I've ever performed. I wiggled around on the floor until I faced the front of the van. I reached forward to the gearshift. Yes, I could pull it into reverse. Since I have long arms, I might even manage to push the accelerator with my hand and back the van up. There was no way of telling what I'd back into, but I didn't see how I'd be any worse off.

I did it. I moved the gearshift into reverse, then leaned forward and pushed the accelerator with my hand. The van seemed to shoot backward. I could feel the flat going bump, bump, bump, and another shot clunked into the van. At least I was able to get a fix on this one. It was coming from the left of the van, and it hit the motor or the fender—something in front of me, anyway.

I kept pushing the accelerator, figuring that anyplace else was better than the place I was in. More shots came, some in the roof, some in the hood. And they definitely came from the left and in front. The shooter obviously couldn't see me. He was just firing at the van. Which still left me in a very sticky spot.

I was beginning to wonder if I could drive clear back to town without looking behind me, when the van jolted to a stop and threw me backward. I looked out the rear window and saw trees. The van had angled into the bushes and trees at the side of the road.

Now what? I didn't have time to think about it. I reached for the dash and hit the button that pops the rear deck. Then I scrambled over the seats to get to the rear of the van. The deck's door had opened, but it hadn't popped up very far, since the trees and bushes had stopped it. I was able to push it up until there was a space at the bottom of a foot or eighteen inches.

All I could see outside was bushes, but that looked better than what was inside. I crawled out headfirst, wriggling through the crack and slithering into the bushes like a snake.

I pulled myself along with my elbows, trying to get deeper into the trees and brush and farther away from the road. Behind me I heard a couple more shots hit metal, and I allowed myself to hope that the rifleman thought I was still inside the van.

I soon felt as if I'd crawled a mile, but when I looked back the van was just about fifteen feet away. I crawled harder.

For the first time in my life, I wished the woods were thicker. I didn't dare stand up for fear I'd be clearly visible. Since I had only a general idea of where the gunman was, I didn't know when he might get a glimpse of my khaki jacket and blond hair moving along. He wasn't likely to mistake me for a woodchuck, though I could hope that my jacket looked like fallen leaves. Or maybe it didn't. I rolled over on my back and wriggled out of the jacket. My green, long-sleeved polo shirt would offer better camouflage, at least for the top half of me. I couldn't do anything about my jeans. I pulled a small branch off a bush and stuck it in the clip that held my hair in a clump at the back of my neck, with the leaves over the back of my head. The branch poked my spine, and I must have looked like a fool, but that didn't seem important.

I left the jacket behind and kept crawling. I wouldn't allow myself to look back for what I thought was a long time. I began to wonder if I could stand up and run for it without getting shot. The wind was whipping the tops of the trees around, but they weren't moving so much down on the ground. When I finally peeked over my shoulder, the van was just a white blob through the trees. I'd crawled fifty or sixty feet.

Then I saw movement near the van. I froze, lying motionless with my nose to the ground.

But what if the rifleman was coming into the woods after me? I couldn't stand not to look. I lifted my head and peered toward the van. All I could see was a dark figure moving beside the van. Then I heard a door open.

The rifleman was looking inside the van. This was my chance. I jumped to my feet, losing the branch I'd used to hide my hair. I ran behind a big tree, an evergreen of some kind. Then I stood still, not daring to breathe, hoping that the wind would make all the trees move enough to hide the way my tree was quaking.

I heard a bang, but it wasn't a shot. The van's door had slammed. Apparently the guy with the rifle hadn't seen my dash.

I moved the branches of the evergreen aside, very gently, willing the dark figure not to see the motion. I could make out the van and the figure, but I couldn't see any detail. It was just a blob moving around. But it could easily move toward me, into the woods.

I didn't dare stay where I was.

I looked for another likely hiding place, one farther from the van. Trees and bushes were all I could see in any direction. I picked a likely tree—another nice, thick evergreen—selected a path to it, and skedaddled. I reached it without any shots being fired. I stood still a minute, then picked another tree that looked as if it could hide a six-foot blond. This one was a maple with lots of bushes around its trunk. I ran for that one. I picked another tree. I ran for it. I kept this up for a long time.

For the first time in my life I subscribed to Aunt Nettie's view that trees were for hiding behind. Unfortunately, I was also highly aware of my own view of trees as hiding places for potential enemies.

But I slogged on, seeking out the thickest bushes and trees I could find for what seemed like hours.

Finally I decided I needed to assess my situation. I looked at my watch, then crawled under the low branches of an evergreen. I was determined to lie still for five whole minutes and try to see if the rifleman was following me.

I couldn't hear anything except my own panting and the wind high in the trees. Had I escaped? I was shivering; I hoped my shaking wouldn't rustle the dry leaves that covered the forest floor. A picture of a forest popped into my mind—a still forest with one tree shaking like mad. The one I was under.

I was so giddy the picture almost made me laugh. I tried to force myself to lie still. This wasn't hide and seek. It wasn't even paintball. It was life or death. My life. My death.

Still I heard nothing. My panting gradually turned into longer breaths. I lay quietly. I counted to two hundred. It had been long enough for me to check my watch, I decided. Surely the five minutes I'd allotted were up. I lifted my head and looked at my wrist.

That's when I realized the next danger I faced. Because now, under the branches of the evergreen, I couldn't read my watch. It was too dark to make out the time. I wouldn't be able to read it until I'd punched the little button that lit up the face. But I knew what time it was.

It was time to panic.

It was nearly dark. I had no idea which way I had run since I fled from the rifleman. The temperature was dropping. And I'd left my jacket under some bush.

I was beginning to believe I'd gotten away from the rifleman, but I might be in as much danger here as I had been in the van. I was lost in the woods with no flashlight and no jacket. And it was getting dark fast.

I crawled out from under the evergreen and stood

up. That was one of the worst moments in my life. Five generations of North Texas ancestors hovered over me, murmuring, "Trees, trees, trees, trees! Trees in every direction. You can't *see* where you're going! You can't *see* the horizon! Nobody's even going to start looking for you until you don't show up for your date with Joe at nine o'clock! You'll be dead by then! They won't find your body until the spring thaw! Animals will gnaw your bones!"

It was all I could do to keep from running off in all directions.

Then a different group of North Texas ancestors began to murmur. "Wait a minute, gal. There may be trees, but east is still east, west is still west, and north and south haven't budged. Dangerous wild animals are scarce in this part of Michigan; this ain't the Upper Peninsula. You might stumble over a skunk or a deer, but they won't eat'cha. You kin git outta this, baby doll."

I took three deep breaths and resolved to start getting out of it while there was at least a glimmer of light coming from the overcast sky.

Speaking of light, that wasn't going to be any help in deciding which way to go. The blankety-blank trees were hiding the sky. I couldn't tell which quadrant was lighter, which way the sun had set.

So I listened. On my left I heard highway noise. That would be the trucks on Interstate 196. On my right I heard Lake Michigan. That cool west wind was whipping the normally placid water into surf. It might not be booming like the Pacific, but it was loud enough to hear.

If the Interstate was on my left, and the lake was on my right, I was facing south. The highway and the lake were usually from a mile to three miles apart. I turned right, toward the lake. If I kept the sound of the highway behind me and walked toward the sound of the surf, I'd be headed due west. I'd eventually hit Lake Shore Drive. The route I'd picked meant I was going to head directly into the wind, but I couldn't help that.

It was getting colder, and the wind cut right through my T-shirt. But I'd be warmer if I kept moving.

I did it. I will say it wasn't easy. Walking through the woods as it gets darker and darker is not fun. But I kept moving toward the sound of the surf.

The terrain in west Michigan isn't hilly. Of course, there were gullies and rises and trees and vines and other stuff I don't want to think about. But I kept moving, with the wind in my face and headed toward the sound of the surf.

Once I fell, slid down a slope, and wound up with my feet in a creek. But it was a sneaker day, so I didn't lose my shoes. I squished up the other side of the creek bank. And when I got to the top, I could hear the lake again. The blessed, beautiful lake. I walked on toward it, placing each foot down carefully to be sure I had a firm place to step before I put any weight on it. A twisted ankle could be fatal.

My teeth were chattering, even before I fell in the creek, and I got colder and colder as I walked. The temptation to step behind a tree and huddle down out of the wind was great. I sure wished I had that khaki jacket I'd abandoned. But that couldn't be helped. I gritted my teeth and kept on walking west. Toward the lake.

The Texas ancestors kept at me. "Come on, baby girl. We fought drought and Comanches and built that little town on the prairie. We didn't do it by giving in. Keep on. One foot in front of the other. Head west. You come from tough stock."

The Dutch side of the family began to lecture me, too. "If you come from tough Texas stock, Susanna

Lee, you come from tough Dutch stock, too. Do you think we had it easy? Leaving a civilized country to settle in the wilds? To be drafted into service in the Civil War when we didn't even speak English? To try to be a skilled woodworker in a place where people built their furniture from logs with the bark still on? To face winters as cold as Holland's without a warm house, without a tile stove? We didn't fear the cold. We kept going. Of course you're cold, but you're a healthy young woman. You'll get to Lake Shore Drive before you get pneumonia."

My first ray of hope arrived when I came to a house. I could see its roof—a straight line where everything else was curved. I burst out of the woods and into a yard.

But there were no lights on and when I walked up to it, I saw—actually felt—that the windows were covered with shutters. It was a summer cottage and was closed for the winter.

At least it would have a drive, a driveway or lane I could follow to Lake Shore Drive. But I circled the house, and I couldn't find the drive. It was too dark to see it.

I almost decided to break into the cottage and wait for morning. But the shutters were nailed on tight, and I didn't have as much as a stick to pry them off.

I listened for the surf, faced west, and slogged on. I climbed up rises and slid down the other side. My wet socks squished inside my wet shoes. I kept the wind in my face and listened for the surf.

And finally, I saw a light.

It was off to my left. As quickly as it appeared, it disappeared. Then it reappeared. I realized it was a stationary light; the blowing branches were making it appear and disappear. I turned toward the light.

I took one more fall, stumbling over a fallen branch and landing on my knees. Then the brush thinned out. I stepped onto sand, then onto asphalt. I had reached Lake Shore Drive.

I threw my head back and yelled. Or I tried to yell. The "Yeehaw!" I had thought would be a victory cry came out as a meek little croak. But I was standing on a paved road. If my feet hadn't been so cold, I would have danced.

I stood there, looking across the road and down about fifty yards to a row of Asian-looking lanterns on top of a wall. I had not only reached Lake Shore Drive, I knew where I was. I was about two miles south of Aunt Nettie's house, across from the Hart compound. I even knew who lived there. Timothy Hart. I felt sure he'd let me use his phone.

For the first time, I began to cry. Rescue was within sight.

I limped toward Timothy Hart's house, breathing a prayer. "Please, God, don't let Timothy be drunk."

I didn't think Timothy would be dangerous, drunk or sober, but approaching the house of a drunk in the dark just didn't seem like a good idea. He might have passed out, for one thing.

But I climbed through the gate, and when I looked at Timothy's little farmhouse, I saw a light in the living room and Timothy walked in front of the window. I couldn't run, but I still made pretty good time getting up those front steps and pounding on the door. And Timothy Hart answered the door, white mustache neat as ever, every beautiful white hair in place. He looked every inch the distinguished older gent. And he was sober.

"Lee! What's happened?"

I fell on his neck. "Oh, Timothy, someone tried to kill me and I had to run through the woods! I'm freezing to death! Can I come in and take off my shoes and call for help?"

After Timothy finished gaping, he took care of me

like a baby. When my fingers were too stiff to untie my wet shoelaces, he took my shoes off for me. He brought me a blanket and wrapped me up. He gave me hot coffee. I accepted all that, but I drew the line at a hot bath.

"I'll wait until I get home," I said. "Can I use your phone?"

"Of course. You should call the police."

"First I'll call Joe."

Timothy patted my shoulder and handed me the telephone. Joe answered his cell phone on the second ring. I began to pour out the whole story. I was sobbing, but I didn't even know it until Timothy handed me a box of tissues.

Then I realized Joe had been trying to say something. I stopped and let him speak. "Where are you?"

"At Timothy Hart's."

"But you said the rifle shots were fired over by Gray Gables."

"Yes. I ran through the woods."

"Through the woods? That's at least two miles."

"Well, I took my time!" I looked at a grandfather clock in the corner of Timothy's living room. It was nearly seven o'clock. "I was running through the woods for two hours!"

"My god, woman!" Joe took a deep breath. "Have you called the cops?"

"Not yet." I sobbed. "I just wanted to talk to you!"

"Listen, don't move. Don't call anybody. Don't do anything. Stay there. I'll call the chief. Then I'll be there."

I barely had time to use Timothy's bathroom before Joe's truck pulled up outside. I hadn't washed my face; I wanted to look as if I'd had a bad experience. Right that moment I wanted sympathy more than I wanted admiration, and I'm delighted to say that Joe provided it. He had called Aunt Nettie, so she arrived as well, and both of them petted me and gave me all the sympathy I could wish for. I was hugged so hard my ribs were sore for a week. However, neither Chief Hogan Jones nor any of his minions came.

"I thought you were going to call the chief," I said.

"I did," Joe said. "He was in Holland having dinner with VanDam. They'll be here in a minute."

I was almost sorry when they did show up, because I had to tell the whole story in an orderly fashion. It took a while to get my thoughts together.

VanDam and Hogan Jones both pressed me on the dark figure I had seen near the van.

"I wish I could tell you something," I said. "It was just a dark figure. Somebody in a hooded jacket or maybe just a sweatshirt. It might not have even been the guy with the rifle. It might have been one of the neighbors over there trying to find out what was going on."

Hogan shook his head. "I don't think so. At least nobody has reported a wrecked or abandoned van over there. It wasn't found until I sent a car over to check."

"I guess my van's a total loss."

Hogan patted my hand. "It may be, Lee. But you're not."

He meant the remark to be comforting, but it sent me into another fit of shivering. I pulled Timothy's blanket tight and turned to Joe for a hug. But the chief motioned, and Joe got up. He, Hogan, and Van-Dam retired to Timothy's kitchen for a conference.

In a moment they came back. Hogan pulled a kitchen chair up close to me, so he could look straight into my face. Joe sat down beside me, and VanDam loomed behind Hogan. I expected Hogan to say, "Here's the plan."

But he didn't. He said, "Okay, Lee. We don't know

who fired those shots at you, but it's very likely it was the same person who tried to shoot Aubrey Andrews Armstrong."

"That makes sense. How many mad riflemen can we have in a town the size of Warner Pier?"

"But we know a little more about him now. He's a local."

"A local?"

"At least he has enough local knowledge to know that TenHuis Chocolade furnishes chocolates to Gray Gables. He knew that if he called in an order you'd run right out there."

"He must have even known that I'm usually the one who makes deliveries."

Hogan nodded. "And he knows you got out of that van alive and crawled off into the bushes."

"Right. So?"

"So let's be cagey here. Let's let the bastard think he killed you."

CHOCOLATE CHAT

PET PROTECTION

Chocolate can be very dangerous to our household pets.

The culprit is theobromine, one of the chemicals found in chocolate. In small amounts, it can cause vomiting and restlessness in pets. Other symptoms of chocolate poisoning are increased respiration, muscle spasms and seizures. Larger amounts can be fatal.

Pure chocolate—baking chocolate, for example—is the most dangerous. Half an ounce of this might kill a small dog, such as a Chihuahua or a toy poodle, while it might take four ounces to be fatal to a large dog, such as an adult Labrador or a collie.

Cats typically have a lower body weight than dogs, and are consequently at even greater risk of theobromine poisoning.

One unexpected source of theobromine? A type of garden mulch, sold commercially by a number of chains, is made from cocoa bean shells. It's good for plants, but could harm pets, so check the ingredients carefully before you buy.

And remember: chocolate people-treats should *always* be kept away from pets.

Chapter 14

"Yeah, Lee," Joe said. "Maybe you could just disappear for a few days."

I barely had to think a minute. "That sounds heavenly," I said.

Yes, at first disappearing sounded like a wonderful idea. But I quickly realized it isn't the easiest thing to do.

Sure, we'd all like simply to retire from the world on occasion. No phone calls, no letters, no e-mail. In fact, people have been known to do that. But those people probably weren't planning to come back. My disappearance had to be short-term, and that's a problem. I mean, when you go on vacation, you stop the newspaper, right? If you just disappear, you can't do that. Newspapers and the other routine matters of life pile up.

My very first comment showed I had the wrong idea. "I guess I could work at home for a few days."

The chief shook his head. "Nope. No work."

"No work? But this is our busy season!"

"Yeah, but nobody's going to believe you're dead if you're still turning out work."

Aunt Nettie spoke. "We could manage, Lee. I could tell you what comes up, you could tell me what to do, and I could do it."

This time the chief smiled as he shook his head. "No, Nettie. You'd have to be away from the office as well. You'd be involved in the search for Lee."

"Oh!" Aunt Nettie gave a little gasp. "I guess you're right. It wouldn't be very realistic for me to keep on making chocolates if Lee were missing."

"That's right," VanDam said. "It will have to be a complete masquerade or there's no point."

We worked on the details. Aunt Nettie and I would stay home twenty-four hours a day. She would answer the phone. If people came to the house—"And they will," Chief Jones warned. "The ghouls will gather."—Aunt Nettie couldn't let them in. If she couldn't avoid letting them in, I'd have to hide out. We'd have to leave most of the shades drawn. Aunt Nettie would have to stay away from the shop.

The worst part was I'd have to let my friends believe something terrible had happened to me.

"How about Lindy? I'd have to tell Lindy," I said.

"Nope." The chief's voice was firm. "And the same with the people at the shop. If they know you're all right, someone is sure to let it slip. The only way is just to disappear, Lee. If you can't do that . . . well, we'll have to think of a different plan."

I was confused. "But what's the point of all this? Why do you want the rifleman to think I'm dead?"

Joe answered. "First off, Lee, it's the best way to keep you safe."

"I appreciate that. But couldn't I just go to a motel in Holland or something? Then I could at least do some work."

"That's an alternative we could consider," Chief Jones said. "But I'd like to try the disappearing act for a few days. It will give us an excuse to search the woods around here thoroughly, for example. We can look in people's outbuildings. And you never know when somebody will say the wrong thing, let something slip."

"What about Timothy?" I said.

We all turned to look at him. Timothy Hart was the weak link in all this, of course. Tim is a sweetheart in a lot of ways, but he had spent years in an alcoholic fog. He's not the person I'd pick to share an important secret.

Timothy drew himself up proudly, then assured us he had been dry for nine months.

"I will not say a word to a soul," he said. "I'll stay home from AA."

"We don't want you to do that," Chief Jones said. "Just remember, Tim, that one dropped hint at the Superette could be fatal for Lee."

Timothy promised silence with great solemnity. But the chief's warning left me more scared than I had been since I fell out of the woods onto Lake Shore Drive. Somehow the chief's comment made the whole thing seem real. Until then it had had a dreamlike quality.

When we got back to Aunt Nettie's house, I did insist that I be allowed to phone my parents in Texas, so I could tell them I was really all right before news of my disappearance hit the news media. It turned out that my mother, who's a travel agent, was in Mongolia, so I called my dad in Prairie Creek, Texas.

As soon as he figured out I was alive and not in need of medical attention, he wanted to know about my van. My dad owns a small garage, and he'd found that van and fixed it up for me.

"I haven't seen it," I said. "It's still sitting over there where the guy with the rifle was. But I'm afraid it's in pretty bad shape, judging from the number of shots it took. I know the windshield's gone, and maybe the tires."

"That's easy to fix," he said.

"I'm sure you and a good body man could get it back in tiptop condition, Dad. But I don't think I'll ask you to try. I never want to see that van again."

I teared up and had to hand the phone to Chief Jones then. The chief warned my dad not to speak to any reporters. "A hint that Lee is alive could mean she's not," he said.

By then I was able to talk again, and I took the phone to say good-bye. "Bye-bye, Daddy. Don't worry about me."

"Take care, honey. I'll do my best to act real natural."

There was no reason to believe the rifleman was watching any of us, but the chief and Lieutenant VanDam were determined to make my disappearance look real. For example, the chief, who must have thought of this plan the minute Joe called him in Holland, had first sent a patrolman in an unmarked car to check out my van. Joe got the job of making the official "discovery" that I was missing.

Joe had said good-bye at Timothy Hart's. Later he told me he stopped and picked up a sandwich, trying to act as if that was the reason he'd been roaming around, then went back to his apartment and cleaned up his painting supplies. At nine p.m. he walked across the street and banged on the door of TenHuis Chocolade, giving an imitation of a guy trying to keep a date.

Meanwhile, I got in and out of the shower. That turned out to be a painful process, since my elbows were skinned worse than when I learned to ride a bike the Christmas I was seven. Aunt Nettie smeared them with antibiotic ointment and covered them with gauze. By the time Joe called the house to complain that I had stood him up, I was tucked into bed in a flannel nightie. I listened on the upstairs extension while Aunt Nettie assured him I hadn't come home.

"Oh, dear, Joe. Where can she be? It's not like her to—well, just disappear."

Joe didn't laugh. "She said something about making a delivery after work."

"That wouldn't have taken her long. She was taking some mints out to Gray Gables."

Joe pretended to think that over. "That end of Inland Road can be pretty lonely this time of year with all the summer cottages closed. I'll drive out there and make sure she didn't have car trouble."

Aunt Nettie made me comfort food—a grilled cheese sandwich, a cup of hot chocolate, and two Mexican vanilla truffles ("Light vanilla interior in milk chocolate.")—and brought it upstairs on a tray. I turned on my dim bedside lamp and ate it. After I finished, I lay down knowing it would be a half hour or more before anything else happened. Joe had to "discover" my van, call the police, and wait for them to arrive before he could call Aunt Nettie again. I guess I fell asleep. I found out later Aunt Nettie had unplugged the upstairs telephone. I slept through most of the night's excitement. I've always suspected Aunt Nettie of dissolving an antihistamine in my hot chocolate.

Aunt Nettie had the hard role, of course. She had to be up all the night, taking calls from the police and acting worried.

The next day was more of the same. I mainly stayed upstairs. Of course, I did have to sneak downstairs to the bathroom now and then, since we only have one. This meant Aunt Nettie had to keep all the downstairs shades pulled. Chief Jones stationed a patrol car in her driveway, ostensibly to keep reporters away, actually to give the two of us warning of visitors.

But the main problem with being a missing person was boredom. By that afternoon I was out of my skull, ready to throw a shoe at the television and all set to trash every book in the house.

I wanted to read the files of the Warner Pier *Gazette,* and I couldn't do that.

I told Joe as much when he came by under the guise of consoling Aunt Nettie.

"I never realized that solitary confinement is cruel and unusual punishment," I said.

"What bothers you the most?"

"I'm *missing* everything! I don't know what's going on."

"The cops are mainly tramping around in the woods," Joe said. "I thought you got enough of that last night."

"I did. But I still want to know what's happening. I had big plans for today."

"Lee, have you been detecting again? Chief Jones said—"

"I wasn't doing anything that any citizen couldn't do. All I'd planned for today was a trip to the *Gazette* office. I was going to look at their files."

"What files?"

"Files on everybody who seemed to be mixed up with Aubrey Andrews Armstrong."

"You mean Maia and Vernon?"

"And Maggie McNutt. And maybe Ken."

"What did they have to do with Armstrong?"

I bit my tongue. I couldn't tell Joe all the details. "Maggie was afraid of him," I said. "She thought he was a crook." I didn't mention seeing the red Volkswagen near the fruit stand just after I found Silas Snow's body.

Joe looked at me and shook his head. "I'll try to find you some new reading material," he said.

But it was Chief Jones who showed up at five p.m. with a large, flat bundle.

Aunt Nettie let him in while I stayed away from

the door. He plunked the bundle on the dining room table. "Here, Lee. Joe says you need something to keep you busy."

"What's that?"

"It's five years' worth of bound Warner Pier *Gazette* copies. It wasn't the easiest thing I ever accomplished, but I pulled rank and got them from the library."

I eyed them suspiciously. "You had to pull rank?"

"They're normally not checked out."

"I know. But what do you want me to do with them?"

"Look through them. See what you find out. About Maia. About Vernon." He waved his hand. "Joe said you'd planned to look the *Gazette* files over."

"Yeah, but Chuck was going to let me see his personal files. I figured they'd be clippings, not whole newspapers."

"I'll go by there tomorrow and photocopy everything in Chuck's files. And I'll let you see it. But they're probably not too complete. It would help me if you'd look through these papers."

I gave the chief a short list of people who had been involved with Aubrey Andrews Armstrong or who had showed any interest in him: Maia, Vernon, Maggie and Ken, Silas Snow himself, maybe Chuck O'Riley—it was hard to go much further than that.

"I guess Silas had a hired man," Aunt Nettie said.

The chief nodded. "Yes, his name is Tomas Gonzales."

I wrote that down, but I didn't expect to stumble over it in the Warner Pier *Gazette*. Except for Mayor Mike Herrera and schoolkids, the Hispanic citizens of Warner Pier tend to be invisible.

The whole thing had the air of a make-work project designed to keep Lee busy and out of the hair of law enforcement. I didn't like it. But I'd agreed to the disappearance, so I could hardly say I was too busy to look at five years of old *Gazettes*.

"I'll start after dinner," I said.

"Oh, my!" Aunt Nettie said. "I forgot to tell you, Lee. Hazel and Dolly insisted on cooking dinner for me. Dolly's supposed to bring it out just after five."

"We'll have to hide these *Gazettes*, then," the chief said.

We barely had time to stow the heavy bound volumes upstairs when our police companion in the driveway beeped his horn to warn us someone was coming. I sat in a comfortable chair in the corner of my room, ready to stay quiet. There are no secrets in Aunt Nettie's house; the smallest whisper or the tiniest creak of a bedspring is heard throughout the house.

Of course, that meant I could also hear every word spoken in the living room. I sat down, picked up my book, and cocked an ear for Dolly Jolly's booming tones.

But the voice of the visitor didn't boom. It tinkled. The visitor and Aunt Nettie had to come right into the living room before I realized who it was. Lindy Herrera.

"This is just unbelievable!" she said. "Who? Who could try to do any harm to Lee?"

She was crying. I felt like such a louse. I nearly got up and went downstairs. But I'd promised the chief that my "disappearance" would last at least two days. I reached for a Kleenex.

Aunt Nettie was sniffling, too. "Lindy, we're not going to lose hope yet. I'm sure this will have a happy ending."

That made Lindy cry harder, of course. I sat there, listening to her grieve and feeling lower than a snake's belly. How did Chief Jones talk me into this? Why did he want me to hide out, anyway? I didn't really have a clear idea.

Lindy only stayed about ten minutes. When she left, Aunt Nettie, still making soothing noises, walked out with her.

I didn't dare peek out the window, but I heard Lindy's car leave, and I heard Aunt Nettie come back in.

She was talking as she came in. I stayed put, afraid that some new visitor had showed up to grieve. But Aunt Nettie wasn't comforting the new visitor. In fact, she was talking rather oddly.

"We'll just put your things in the corner of the dining room," she said. "I'll get you some dinner. Then we'll settle down for a quiet evening."

I heard some shuffling around, but nobody replied. Then Aunt Nettie spoke again. "Oh, all right. If you want me to, I'll scratch your tummy."

Chapter 15

It was Monte. Lindy had brought the chocolate Labrador puppy back.

Was she insane? How could Aunt Nettie and I take care of a dog? Had Lindy left? Was it safe for me to go down and ask just what was going on?

Aunt Nettie called up the stairs, answering my question. "Lee, you can come down now."

I thudded down to the living room, and Monte greeted me joyfully, running in circles, snuffling at my feet, and barking a welcome. "Monte! I thought you were safe at the vet's!"

"Lindy's vet doesn't board dogs," Aunt Nettie said. "He called her today and said someone would have to pick up Monte. So she did. She was going to keep him at her house, but after the poisoning episode she was afraid to do that. Besides, she and Tony are at work and the kids are at school all day, so there was nobody to look after Monte. She was going to put him in a boarding kennel, but I thought it would be better to have him here."

"Why?"

Aunt Nettie's face screwed up. "Oh, he's such a nice little dog! He needs more attention. Being in a kennel—Lee, you were complaining about being in solitary confinement. Why would we wish that on Monte? After all, we're both here."

"But I can't go outside to walk him."

"It won't hurt me to walk him. Or we'll get the patrolman to help us."

The patrolman's warning horn beeped. Another car was coming. "That must be Dolly with dinner," Aunt Nettie said.

I ran for the stairs. Monte barked and followed me, scrambling up the stairs. I settled myself in my little room with Monte in my lap. If I made a noise, at least Aunt Nettie would have the dog to blame.

A few moments later Dolly's voice boomed beneath me. "No word yet?"

"Not yet, Dolly. I'm considering that good news. How did the day go at the shop?"

"Fine! Fine! We got the Whole Foods order off! Have the police given you any hint of what could have happened to Lee?"

"Not really, Dolly. They say there was no blood in her car. That's a good sign."

I heard a loud creak, and I recognized it as the noise an old wicker rocking chair makes when someone heavy sits in it. I gathered Dolly had sat down. When she spoke again her voice barely boomed. She sounded extremely depressed.

"Nettie, I'm so afraid I could be partly responsible for—for whatever has happened to Lee."

"Whatever do you mean?"

"If I could just be *sure!*"

"Sure of what? Dolly, if you know anything about this attack on Lee, you've got to tell Chief Jones or the state policeman."

"I don't know anything, really! I just suspect!" Listening to Dolly's voice, I could picture the misery on her broad, freckled face. "It seems like the act of a madman. And there's a person around here I feel sure is crazy!"

Aunt Nettie gave an impatient snort. "I could name more than one, Dolly. But whoever lured Lee out to Gray Gables was smart, you know. It wasn't just a random act of violence. He went to a lot of trouble to get her out there—faking a phone call. Putting nails in the road so she'd have a flat. It doesn't seem crazy."

"Crazy like a fox!"

"Maybe so. If you have any specific suspicions we'll call that patrolman who's outside in the driveway. He'll get Chief Jones on the radio and call him back here so you can tell him."

"It's too humiliating!"

"Humiliating!" I could hear the anger in Aunt Nettie's voice. She rarely gets angry, but when she does, look out. She might be half Dolly's size and her voice might be a third the decibel level, but when she's stirred up I'll put my money on Aunt Nettie against a horde of cannibals brandishing spears.

And at that moment Aunt Nettie was definitely stirred up. "Dolly, if you're keeping some knowledge away from the police because you're afraid it will *embarrass* you—well, you're not the woman I thought you were! I won't stand by and let you get away with that! You won't have to wait on the police to get the third degree! I'll give it to you myself!"

"Oh, Nettie, I don't know a thing about Lee!

"Then what do you know?"

"All I know is what became of Dennis Grundy!"

Dennis Grundy? I couldn't believe I'd heard right. What on earth could Dennis Grundy have to do with some guy shooting at me with a rifle?

I guess Aunt Nettie felt the same way, because she yelled out words that echoed what I was thinking.

"Dennis Grundy! Dennis Grundy? Who cares about Dennis Grundy?"

"Dennis Grundy was murdered!"

"I don't care! He has nothing to do with Lee."

"That's what I'm afraid the police will say!"

Aunt Nettie was silent a moment. She wasn't yelling when she went on. "Dolly, just what do you know about Dennis Grundy? And why do you think it matters?"

There was more sniffling from Dolly. Then she spoke loudly.

"The Snows killed him!"

"What? I thought he ran off with the daughter—Julia."

"No! That's what they let everybody think. But they really killed him."

"Why?"

"Oh, it was like a shotgun wedding that didn't come off, I guess. Julia was pregnant. He wasn't ready to marry her. Somehow he wound up dead."

"What became of Julia?"

"She went to a home for unwed mothers. She was angry with her family! She hated her father! She never went home!"

Finally Aunt Nettie got around to the question I'd been dying to ask. "How do you know all this?"

"Julia Snow was my grandmother!"

Dolly Jolly must have been completely deaf if she didn't hear the gasp I gave. It must have reverberated right through the floor of my bedroom and on through the ceiling of the living room. Dolly was the granddaughter of the heroine of Maia's cornball novel? Dolly was a relative of Silas Snow and of Maia Michaelson? It was hard to believe.

"That's the real reason I came to Warner Pier. I wanted to know more about the Snow family." Dolly gave a gasp louder than mine. "Oh, Nettie! You won't tell Maia!"

"I won't tell anybody, Dolly. But why do you think it has any connection to our current problems?"

"Because there must be a streak of insanity in the Snow family! Maia must be the one who killed Silas. Her own uncle! And now she's attacked Lee. She must be crazy! Maybe I'm crazy, too!"

Aunt Nettie immediately began to concentrate on calming Dolly, assuring the red-haired giantess that she seemed to be perfectly sane.

Dolly gave a brief outline of what had become of Julia Snow. Julia had gone to a home for unwed mothers and had given Dennis Grundy's baby up for adoption. She had moved to Detroit, where she found a job in a bakery. She married a fellow baker and they had a successful business. She had only one other child, Dolly's mother.

Julia had kept quiet about her youthful indiscretions until her last illness five years earlier, during which Dolly had helped nurse her. Then she had rambled on to her granddaughter, giving Dolly a confused account of her early life.

"Gramma was really confused at the end, but she always claimed her family killed Dennis Grundy," Dolly said. "She wasn't always clear about which one had done it. Her father seemed most likely. I always thought she didn't really know. But after she died— well, I thought I'd come over here and find out what kind of people the Snows were. And I think they're all crazy!"

Aunt Nettie continued to assure Dolly that the Snows might be crazy, but Dolly didn't seem to have taken after them. She left after about fifteen minutes, promising that she'd contact Chief Jones.

That fifteen minutes gave me time to think over Dolly's story, and after that brief reflection I didn't think much of it. It was startling to learn that Dolly was a descendant of Julia Snow, who had been a central character in a Warner Pier legend. And even more startling to learn that Julia had claimed that her family killed her lover, Dennis Grundy.

But what could that possibly have to do with the things that had happened that week? Silas Snow had been beaten to death with a shovel behind his own fruit stand. Aubrey Andrews Armstrong had been the target of a rifleman, then had disappeared leaving all his belongings including his cherished pet behind, and becoming himself a suspect in the death of Silas Snow. And then the rifleman had apparently tried to kill me.

I couldn't see any connection between those events and the seduction of a country girl by a small-time gangster seventy-five years earlier.

Dolly's theory seemed to be that Maia was some kind of homicidal maniac. I didn't believe it.

Of course, I couldn't believe Maggie or Ken McNutt or anybody else I knew—including Aubrey Andrews Armstrong—could be guilty, either. The whole situation was unbelievable.

I heard Dolly's Volkswagen bus drive down the lane, and I slowly came downstairs. I found Aunt Nettie in the kitchen, frowning.

"What did you make of all that stuff Dolly was handing out?" I asked.

"You heard?"

"Yes, but I don't really understand."

"I didn't either. I just hope that Dolly goes straight to Chief Jones and doesn't go around town dropping hints. She could put herself in danger."

"True. But I heard her promise to go to the chief. What about Maia—do you think she's a mad killer?"

Aunt Nettie poured a plastic dish of green beans into a saucepan and put it on the stove. "It seems like a silly idea. Of course, I keep thinking of the old Maia, before she was an author." She gestured at the saucepan. "Hazel and Dolly sent green beans, mashed potatoes, and a small pork loin. Everything is in the oven but the green beans. There's certainly plenty for both of us."

"I'll set the table. And after dinner I'll get started on the old *Gazette*s."

The bound *Gazette*s turned out to be something of a physical challenge. They were hard to read. A bound newspaper, even a tabloid-sized one like the *Gazette*, comes in a big, awkward book filled with smudged type. The best light in Aunt Nettie's house is in the dining room, and I needed to read upstairs, so that I wouldn't have to hastily hide the big books and myself if someone came to the door. But we were trying to keep the upstairs dark, so it would look as if no one was up there. We couldn't set up a bright light there. We finally improvised some window coverings with old army blankets and put up a card table with a good reading lamp in the room across the hall from mine.

Aunt Nettie gave the blankets a final twitch. "There! Good luck."

"I still feel as if I've been given a make-work project to keep me out of trouble."

"I hope it works. You've already been in enough trouble to last a lifetime."

I'd barely opened the first book, however, when Joe showed up. He brought along a long tube. "A gift from the chief," he said.

"And what is it?"

He popped the end off the tube and pulled out a cylinder of paper. "It's a map."

"More research?"

"To help with the newspapers. He's interested in all the neighbors around here. Anybody who could have fired that shot at Armstrong, then escaped on foot."

"But Joe, even if the rifleman escaped on foot, he could have had a car stashed in any driveway along Lake Shore Drive. There's so much traffic along there no one would have noticed."

"True. But the neighbors have to be investigated."

Joe and I spread the map out on the card table and looked at it. "The chief has marked Dennis Grundy's cottage with an X," Joe said.

"I see it. Where is that in relation to Aunt Nettie's house?"

Joe pointed to it. "Yikes!" I said. "I thought the Grundy cottage was at least a mile south of Aunt Nettie's. But it's lots closer than that."

"More like a half mile," Joe said. "If you go by the back road."

"That means we're a lot closer to Maia and Vernon, too. And to Silas Snow's fruit stand. Since the Grundy cottage is on the Snow place."

"Of course that's a big farm."

"Yes, but it's near the Haven Road exit, and Aunt Nettie's way north of that. I thought since it was a mile on the Interstate, it must be a mile on Lake Shore Drive."

"Actually, the Interstate curves, so it's all in a sort of horseshoe. The two properties are lots closer by way of Lake Shore Drive. And even closer than that if you cut down this road." He peered closely at the map. "It's named Mary Street. I didn't know it existed."

"I didn't, either," I said. "It's those trees. They get me all confused. I can't tell directions."

Then I remembered how I'd told directions the night before. By ear. Traffic behind me, surf in front. I shuddered. Joe put his arms around me. We stood there awhile, and I had a good cry on Joe's shoulder. He didn't say anything.

Then Aunt Nettie called up the stairs. "I walked

the dog, and put him in his crate. Now I'm going to bed! Good night, you two."

I lifted my head. "Good night, Aunt Nettie!"

Joe called out, too. "Good night!" Then he kissed my forehead. "I guess I'd better go."

I put my arms around him. "I don't want you to," I said.

He gave a rueful laugh, but he kept holding me. "With a cop outside in the drive and Aunt Nettie downstairs?"

"I don't care. I want you to stay."

I talked him into it. At least he stayed a long time. When I woke up at four a.m. he was there, but at six he'd gone. He left a note. All it said was, "I love you." That's all it needed to say.

Aunt Nettie and I both got up at our usual times, but we had a leisurely breakfast. She'd just made a second pot of coffee at nine o'clock when our cop companion beeped his horn and Chief Jones's car pulled into the drive. He stopped and talked to the patrol officer who had wasted his time in our driveway. I figured the officer was telling him Joe had stayed nearly all night. I still didn't care.

The chief looked solemn as he came in. "Morning, Nettie. Lee."

Aunt Nettie smiled. "Good morning, Hogan. Do you want a cup of coffee?"

"Maybe. I've just got a minute. But I have to tell you two one bit of news."

The chief was so serious that his comment made my stomach go into a spasm of fear.

Aunt Nettie looked stricken. "What's happened?"

"Nothing, maybe. But we found Aubrey Andrews Armstrong's SUV this morning."

Chapter 16

"Oh, Hogan! Is he dead?"

"He's still missing, Nettie. He wasn't in the SUV."

I jumped into the conversation. "Where was the SUV?"

"In a creek bed off the road to the winery."

"Then it wasn't in our neighborhood."

The chief screwed his face up. "Depends on how you look at it. Where's that map I sent out?"

Aunt Nettie and I led the chief up to the spare bedroom, where the map was laid out on the bed. We all gathered around it, and the chief pointed with a ballpoint pen. "Here's the Grundy cottage. Here's Silas Snow's fruit stand." The pen swooped. "Here's the Interstate." The pen moved east of the Interstate, then tapped. "And here's where the SUV was found."

"Gee," I said. "When you look at from a bird's angle, the winery road is real close. But if we want to buy a bottle of Lake Michigan Red, we have to go way around because we can't cross the Interstate."

"That's true if you drive. But Jerry Cherry tells me that when he was a kid he used to cross the Interstate through culverts and under bridges."

"Then you think someone who lives here on Lake Shore Drive could have ditched the SUV, then walked home?"

"Sure. Or they could have ditched it and someone picked them up."

I left it to Aunt Nettie to make the next comment. "You mean Aubrey, don't you? Aubrey could have ditched his own SUV and had some confederate pick him up."

"Anything's possible, Nettie." The chief gestured at me. "Lee's escape through the woods night before last proves that people can roam around this area at will without being seen. If you look at this map, you can see how many houses there are. You'd think Lee wouldn't have been able to walk even a quarter of a mile without falling into somebody's backyard." He tapped the map again. "But here's Gray Gables, and here's the Hart compound. It's more than a mile, and Lee walked it without stumbling into an occupied house."

"I wanted to find one, too," I said.

"You made that expedition through a heavily wooded area, Lee. We retraced your steps with dogs, and you went over some pretty rough terrain. But my point is that people can move around out here without being seen. So finding Armstrong's SUV in a certain spot doesn't incriminate—or clear—anybody. Including Armstrong himself."

Aunt Nettie pressed coffee on the chief, and he took a cup with him as he left. His last instructions were to me. "Good luck with those old *Gazette*s," he said. "Joe said you thought it was make-work. But it needs to be done, and we don't have anybody available to do it. You might find out something that is key to this whole deal." He walked on toward his car, then turned back. "Don't forget to check the land transfers."

So I got dressed and started in on the *Gazette*s, working backward from the most recent issues and referring to the list of names the chief had brought. By lunchtime I knew a lot about our neighbors.

I knew that the Baileys, who lived closest to Aunt Nettie, had gone to the Bahamas last winter and that their son had been promoted to first sergeant in the U.S. Army. I knew about the Bahamas, of course, since I'd picked up their mail. But neither of them had mentioned the son's promotion, and I hadn't read about it earlier. I found out that Silas Snow had sold thirty acres of orchard land to a developer from Grand Rapids. By cross-checking with the map, I figured out that this plot was farther down Lake Shore Drive, nowhere near the Grundy cottage or the fruit stand. I discovered that Chuck O'Riley had come to Warner Pier because he had relatives in the area; he was the nephew of a Mrs. Vanlandingham who owned an antique shop in Warner Pier.

These discoveries showed the difference between the Warner Pier *Gazette* and a city paper. None of these items would have appeared in the *Dallas Morning News*, or even in the *Grand Rapids Press* or the *Holland Sentinel*. But the *Gazette* would print nearly any news release sent to it, and it loved any type of personal news: college students who made the dean's list, church suppers, club fund-raisers, land transfers. The only two newspapers I ever saw report land sales were the *Gazette* and the *Prairie Creek Press*, back in my Texas hometown, which is about the size of Warner Pier.

I kept on skimming through the *Gazette*s. Ken McNutt, I learned, had taken first prize at an antique car competition, being recognized for the excellent mechanical condition of his red 1959 Volkswagen. The son of the Wilsons, another set of Aunt Nettie's neighbors, had won a scholarship to Perdue. Sally Holton, who lived in a spectacular house right on the lake, had been a hostess for the garden tour of the Warner County League of Garden Clubs. Vernon Ensminger had written an angry letter to the editor, complaining about our state representative's stands on wildlife conservation. "An intelligent policy does not pit hunters against 'tree-huggers,'" he wrote. "No one loves the outdoors and the beauties of nature like hunters. We're the ones who get out to enjoy them and who encourage our families to learn about birds and animals." I knew my dad, also a deer hunter, would endorse his position.

The *Gazette* is just a weekly, of course, and I was able to read at a pretty good rate, once I'd figured out how to recognize a piece contributed by the State Department of Agriculture or by General Motors. Those weren't going to have any local names. And a lot of the articles were already familiar, since I do read the rag, known informally as the "Warner Pier Gaggette," every week.

I got back to early summer when I hit a really interesting article—Chuck's interview with Maia Michaelson, published when her book came out. In it she described her early writing as "a secret vice." She had deliberately kept her ambition to be an author a secret, she had told Chuck. "No one knew of my hidden life but my dear husband, Vernon," she said. "He has been a wonderful help and encouragement to me."

How had she learned to write? "If I have a talent, it's simply a God-given gift," Maia said. "I simply tune in to the eternal. My characters speak to me. Sometimes I feel that I am simply channeling their words, their hopes, and their longings."

Chuck pressed her on how her skills were developed, asking if she had taken writing classes. "Oh, no!" Maia said. "Inspiration can not be regimented! Writing to please a professor would smother the creative impulse."

It made me glad I'm an accountant. We learn our professional skills from people who have already figured out standard ways to perform our required chores. We don't have to start from scratch and teach ourselves—with or without "creative impulse."

But the interview also made me doubt the news Dolly had given me about Maia's publisher. Dolly had been sure that the publishing house did nothing but vanity publications. Maia, however, gave Chuck a whole paragraph about how she had submitted her manuscript to the editor, how she had waited with bated breath, praying that it would be accepted, and how she had greeted the news with ecstasy.

"When I heard from them, I didn't know whether I should laugh or cry," she said. "I danced all around the house!"

That didn't sound as if the editor's acceptance had included a bill for several thousand dollars. Maybe Dolly was wrong.

Maybe that should be checked out. I had Aunt Nettie call the chief. Luckily she had the number of his cell phone. After she handed the phone to me, I quickly sketched Dolly's belief that the publisher of Maia's book only did vanity publishing, contrasting this with Maia's account of selling her book.

"It may not have anything to do with anything," I said, "but it's a little discrepancy, and that's what you said you were interested in."

"Joe's working for me full time," Hogan said. "I'll get him to check it out."

Aunt Nettie again spent the morning answering phone calls from concerned friends. The chief still

had a Warner Pier patrolman stationed in the driveway to keep people from approaching the house, but
the phone rang and rang. Aunt Nettie brought me a
sandwich at noon, and I kept reading. By then I was
back more than a year—like I said, once I learned
which articles to check, I could go through a *Gazette*
pretty fast.

I made sure I looked through the obituaries and
checked the names of survivors. The Snows and Ensmingers had faced another family funeral, I learned,
when a cousin had died a little more than a year ago.
She'd lived at South Haven, but the *Gazette* ran the
obituary because she was originally from Warner
Pier. Or I guess that was the reason. Tracy Roderick
had lost a relative, too—her grandfather. Her mother
was listed among the survivors of a "leading Warner
County fruit farmer" six months earlier. Tracy herself
had been in the paper a lot, because of her class
activities. Most students at WPHS were.

Another source of local names, I discovered, was
activities of the various planning commissions in the
county. I remembered that the Baileys had tried to
build a rental unit on their property. The commission
said no.

Actually, the two square miles I was studying had
come before the township or village planning and
zoning bodies fairly often. Property values in the area
had skyrocketed in recent years, and developers were
trying to buy up property and put in whole addi-
tions. Mostly the commissions hadn't agreed to this,
though one new addition with about twenty-five lots
had been approved. I already knew this; when the
wind was from the east, I could hear the dirt-moving
equipment from my bedroom.

By then I was two years back, to a time before I
moved to Warner Pier. Another developer, I learned
from the *Gazette*s, had applied for permission to de-

velop forty acres closer to Aunt Nettie's house. I
checked the location, and it was right next to the
Grundy cottage. Hmmm, I thought, Silas could have
sold another piece of property—just the way he'd
sold the one farther south—and made a bundle.

I was surprised when I read that he had opposed
the addition. In fact, he'd not only come before the
township commission to speak against it, he'd stated
that he was refusing an offer from the developer.

"That land's been in my family for more than a
hundred years," Silas told the commission. "It's good
orchard land. It would be an out-and-out crime to
cut down those trees and wreck that farmland. I
won't go along with it."

Silas's refusal to sell forced the developer to limit
the size of the project, and the commission turned
the deal down, saying they didn't want the area developed piecemeal.

This episode seemed weird. Silas hadn't objected
to development a mile south. Why had he sabotaged
it there? I turned to the map again.

The plot the developer had tried to subdivide was
just south of the Grundy cottage. He must have
wanted to buy the cottage and the orchard behind it,
where the rifleman had hidden and shot at Aubrey.

I gnawed a knuckle and thought about the Grundy
cottage. Why wouldn't Silas sell it? He didn't rent it
out. He could have torn it down and added the lot
to his orchards, but he hadn't done that, either. He
just let it sit. That didn't seem like wise use of his
resources, but he had the reputation of being a sharp
businessman. I wondered idly just what Vernon and
Maia would do with it.

Aunt Nettie had been not only answering the
phone but also entertaining Monte. Now he came
lumbering into the room on his big puppy feet, looking for a little attention from me. I got up, found an

old sock, and played tug of war with him for a little bit. When he tired I gave him the sock to chew on, sat down, and ate my leftover from lunch—a mocha pyramid bonbon ("Milky coffee interior in a dark chocolate pyramid.").

That chocolate, I remembered, was Maggie McNutt's favorite. I decided to skip ahead in the *Gazette*s, back to the September she and Ken were hired. In a town the size of Warner Pier, new teachers are always profiled. It took me only a few minutes to find the headline: FIVE NEW TEACHERS JOIN WP FACULTY RANKS.

Chuck hadn't been editor in those days, but the story was strictly routine, obviously taken from the resumes of all the new teachers.

Ken, I learned, had received a bachelor's in math from Kalamazoo College, then had gotten a master's in education at the University of Michigan. He'd been a member of the mathematics honorary society and the Young Conservatives. Throughout the first paragraph, his background seemed as nerdy as Ken looked and acted.

Then I came to the second paragraph. "Before attending college," the article said, "McNutt served four years in the U.S. Marine Corps."

The marine corps? I was stunned. Ken looked as if a twenty-mile hike would do him in. How had he managed the marine corps?

The article concluded with a list of Ken's marine corps experiences. He'd served in the artillery section of the marines, and he'd been stationed in the Mideast, as well as several places in the United States. He'd even earned medals.

And one of them was for marksmanship.

Wow. Not only was Ken a much tougher guy than he looked, he was certified as a rifle shot.

Of the people I'd been looking over, two took part

in activities involving rifles. Vernon was an avid deer hunter—even writing letters to the editor about the sport—and Ken a former marine who had earned medals for marksmanship.

And Ken had been near the Grundy cottage the afternoon when someone shot at Aubrey.

But my stomach went into two knots. I liked Ken. I didn't want him to be involved in all this mess— Silas's death, Aubrey's disappearance, the attack on me.

I got so excited that I jumped to my feet and paced up and down. This convinced Monte that I was ready to play again. Maybe I was. A little exercise with a rolled-up sock got me calmed down, but it made Monte whimper and head for the back door. Aunt Nettie took him for a walk around the yard, and I went back to my reading. Having learned the scoop on Ken, I was eager to find out about Maggie.

But I didn't learn much more than I already knew. She and I were pretty good friends. In fact, I would have sworn that Maggie's life was an open book. She was ready to talk about anything—her family, her college years, her time in California. I would have thought I knew all there was to know about her.

Then she'd told me about that threat from Aubrey, his warning that he could blackmail her if she told anybody about him. I still hadn't figured that one out.

But the story in the *Gazette* simply recapped things I already knew. Maggie had studied drama at Northwestern. She had worked in California for seven years. She had returned to the University of Michigan to earn her master's degree. Her hobbies were birding, decorating, and baking bread.

While in California, Maggie had worked at the Pasadena Playhouse and had roles in several films. A list of the films followed.

And one of them was a western. I'd seen it. It was about a wagon train of women, left alone by the men of their party, who withstood an Indian attack. It had been a real shoot-'em-up.

Did that mean Maggie had learned to shoot a rifle?

Well, so what? I had fired a twenty-two myself. My Texas cousin, thrilled with the rifle he'd gotten for his sixteenth birthday, had taken me out to show me his prowess at knocking cans off fence posts. He condescendingly gave me a turn. He wasn't a bit pleased when I could destroy tin cans as well as he could.

I paced the bedroom floor again. I liked Ken. I liked Maggie. I considered them close friends. I did not want close friends involved. I wanted the villain to be Aubrey or some unknown cohort he had brought to Warner Pier. I wanted this crime wave to be the fault of outsiders, not hometown folks.

But just after I had found Silas Snow's body, I had almost run into the red Volkswagen with a WPHS sticker in the back window. There was a ninety percent chance that that car had been driven by either Ken or Maggie.

I just had to ask Maggie if she had been out there or not.

I walked into the next room, checked my purse for Maggie's cell phone number, then punched it in. I was so intent on reaching Maggie that someone answered the phone before I remembered I was supposed to be dead.

Chapter 17

To make things worse, the person who answered the phone was Tracy Roderick.

I made some sound—half snort and half gasp—and hung up.

Whew. That was a narrow escape. Tracy would have recognized my voice after one syllable.

But I did want to talk to Maggie. Did I have to run it through Chief Jones? Or could I simply get Aunt Nettie to summon Maggie and Ken to the house and question them for me? Besides, wasn't it time I was found, safe? Being a missing person was beginning to give me a severe case of cabin fever.

I was still standing there with my hand on the telephone when it rang again. I jumped a mile. After climbing down from the ceiling, I realized I had picked up the receiver, since I had it my hand when I jumped and it was still there when I came down. Luckily, I hadn't made a noise, and I had the presence of mind to keep quiet while Aunt Nettie answered the kitchen phone.

Her voice was cautious. "Hello."

"Oh, Mrs. TenHuis! Have they found Lee?" The voice was Tracy's.

"I don't know anything new, Tracy. I'm sorry."

"I just had the weirdest experience, Mrs. TenHuis. I'm at play rehearsal—"

"At the high school?"

"Yes. I'm at play rehearsal, and I was sitting beside Mrs. McNutt's cell phone, and it just rang. And whoever it was didn't say anything. They just hung up. But it was so weird!"

"Why? It must have been a wrong number."

"I know it's crazy, but . . . you know that little noise Lee makes sometimes? Like when her computer acts up? A kind of a disgusted sniffle?"

"I think I know what you mean, Tracy."

"Whoever called made exactly that noise! Mrs. TenHuis, I just know it *meant* something! You know! I just feel sure it meant Lee's all right!"

I stood there holding the telephone, and I didn't know whether to laugh or cry. I felt awful because I was fooling Tracy, making her worry because she thought I was missing in very suspicious circumstances. At the same time, her gushing conclusions about the "message" my snort had given were hilarious. I covered the receiver and shook all over, trying to stifle my laughter.

Tracy was talking again. "Mrs. TenHuis, I said a prayer for Lee. I just know the Lord will help you find her."

Aunt Nettie's voice was kind. "Tracy, I really appreciate that. You're a lovely young woman, and your prayers are really important."

"Well, Lee really makes working at TenHuis Chocolade fun. And I appreciated her helping me with my hair. But it's just so weird. First Mr. Armstrong disappears. Then Lee. It's as if there's some mal . . . mal . . . mal-violent force at work."

Tracy's spin on "malevolent" made me feel better about my own twisted tongue.

After a few more soothing words from Aunt Nettie, Tracy hung up. I was still standing there with the receiver in my hand when Aunt Nettie also hung up. But I had stopped laughing. I was crying. I just had to be found alive—quick. From the chief's standpoint, my disappearance might be helping solve the case. But it was making all my friends dreadfully unhappy.

And I was just beginning to realize how many friends I had.

I sat down on my unmade bed, found a tissue in the box on the bedside table, wiped my eyes, and blew my nose. I heard Aunt Nettie coming up the stairs, and I didn't even jump up and make the bed. I just left it unmade, the tumbled sheets and blankets clearly showing it had been occupied by two people.

Aunt Nettie poked her head into the room. "Did you hear Tracy?"

"Yes. I feel terrible. We've got to tell Hogan that this disappearance isn't working. It's just too hard on people."

"He's supposed to come by later. We can carry on until then, I guess. Did you call Maggie?"

"Yes. Like an idiot."

"It's lucky you didn't say something, instead of just sniffing."

"I know! Poor Tracy would have known my voice in a minute. She would have thought I was a voice from the beyond and planned a seance."

"Why did you call?"

"I thought of something I wanted to ask Maggie, and I just automatically picked up the phone. I completely forgot I was on the missing list."

"Why did you want to talk to Maggie?"

"About her alibi, I guess."

"Alibi? For what?"

"It doesn't matter. I'll figure another way to approach it. I guess I'd better get back to my *Gazettes*."

"And I'll get back to Monte. I think he wants to go out and play. Again."

Aunt Nettie went back downstairs. For a moment I envied her. It was a beautiful day, though the wind seemed to be turning to the north. At least she got to go outside. I was cooped up in a room with heavy blankets on the windows. And I was itching to talk to Maggie.

I began to make the bed, and I found dark hair on one of the pillows. Which naturally brought me a few fond memories of Joe.

"Joe!" I said aloud. "Joe could call Maggie for me."

There was one catch in that. I couldn't ask Joe to question Maggie without telling him why I thought it would be important to find out if Maggie had been near Silas's fruit stand at the time the old man was killed. I couldn't ask him to question her without revealing that Maggie had a link with Aubrey. And I'd promised Maggie I wouldn't tell anybody—*anybody*—that he was threatening to blackmail her.

The whole thing was a mess, and I'd walked right into it on my own two feet by trying to protect Maggie and Ken.

When Ken had driven by in the red Volkswagen, I could have immediately said, "Gee, I think that's the car I nearly ran into near Silas's fruit stand right after I found his body." If I had, then Hogan Jones could have called Maggie and Ken as a matter of routine and asked if they'd been out near the fruit stand. But if I brought it up now, the chief was going to want to know why I hadn't mentioned it earlier. I didn't want to tell him I hadn't wanted to link Maggie to Aubrey in even a remote way.

"Why?" he'd ask. "Why didn't you tell me you saw that Volkswagen near Silas's fruit stand?"

I'd answer, "Until I saw Ken out at the Grundy cottage in the red VW, I didn't realize that's who I'd seen."

"Why didn't you tell me after you saw Ken in the red Volkswagen?"

"Because right after I saw him, before I had a chance to tell anybody anything, someone took a shot at Aubrey."

"So?"

"Well." I pictured myself fumbling around for an answer. "Because I didn't want you to know there was any link between Maggie and Aubrey."

"And why shouldn't I know that?"

And the only good answer I could have would be, "Because Aubrey was blackmailing her, and that makes it look as if she had a motive for doing him harm."

Maggie did have a motive to wishing Aubrey harm, and therefore Ken did, too. Maybe it was time I let Maggie answer for herself. And let Ken answer for himself. I couldn't imagine what either of them could have had to do with Silas Snow.

In fact, I couldn't picture Maggie doing anything to hurt anyone. But I wasn't so sure about Ken, at least since I discovered he had been a marine. Ken had enough training to know how to kill someone. And I was beginning to suspect Ken might have a lot of hidden depths.

I had boxed myself in. I couldn't avoid telling the chief about Maggie's link to Aubrey, though I didn't have the faintest idea of how that could link to Silas, and a link to Silas seemed to be part of the mix.

I gave up. This was too confusing for me. I was simply going to have to turn it over to Chief Jones. I went downstairs and asked Aunt Nettie to call him.

Her eyes got wide. "What's wrong?"

"I just thought of something I need to tell him." I went back upstairs to my *Gazettes*, feeling glum. I

ground my teeth as I heard Aunt Nettie on the telephone, and my heart sank a few minutes later, when
I heard a car door slam outside. I heard a low male
voice downstairs and I listened for footsteps on the
stairs, dreading to see the chief walk through the
door of Aunt Nettie's extra bedroom.

But the chief didn't come to the door. Joe did.

I jumped up. "I am really glad to see you!"

He gave me a long kiss before he spoke. "I'm glad
to see you, too." He nuzzled my ear. "I sure hated
to leave this morning."

"I was sorry you did. I don't think Aunt Nettie
would have minded if you'd stayed for breakfast.
But that's not why I'm glad to see you. I mean, it's
not the only reason."

"That's not very complimentary."

"Sorry. But I've got to talk to Chief Jones, and I
guess I need moral support."

"He couldn't come right away, so I told him I'd
fill in. What's up."

I sighed and outlined the whole situation. I tried
holding back Maggie's admission that Aubrey had
some hold over her, but Joe went into his attorney
mode and began to cross-examine me.

I tried not to answer. "I don't want to break Maggie's configuration!"

That stopped Joe for a couple of beats, but he figured it out. "Confidence? You don't want to break
Maggie's confidence?"

I nodded miserably.

We were sitting face-to-face in the only two chairs
in the room. He took me by the upper arms and
pretended to shake me. "Don't you realize somebody
tried to kill you?"

"Believe me, I realize it! I've got the scratches and
bruises to remind me."

"And you're still trying to protect people?"

"Joe, I feel sure Maggie didn't have anything to do with this."

"She probably didn't. But the chief still has to talk to her. If she was out there by Silas Snow's fruit stand—"

"*If* that was her car I nearly ran into."

"What if she saw somebody else's car out there, Lee? We've got to ask her. She might not know a thing. But any little crumb of information could help matters."

"Maybe I could just tell her the whole thing's going to come out, give her a chance to come forward and tell the chief on her own."

Joe thought. I could tell that's what he was doing, because he took the opportunity to gnaw on his thumbnail. He has hands like a boat repairman—all banged up—and he bites his nails. Other than that, he's perfect. Or he would be if he didn't want to get married.

Resisting the temptation to get a nail file and start giving him a manicure, I sat quietly until he spoke again. "Maybe we could talk to Maggie. Or I could, I guess. I could tell her to go see the chief."

"I'd feel so much better about doing it that way, Joe."

We went into my room, and Joe called Maggie's cell phone number. We both put an ear to the phone. This time Maggie answered her own phone. First Joe had to answer questions Maggie had about my disappearance. There was nothing new, he told her.

"Listen, Maggie," Joe said. "There's one other thing. Lee told me that the night she found Silas Snow's body, she saw your car out there by his fruit stand."

"Oh!" Maggie sounded startled. "I didn't know anybody saw me."

"She wasn't sure it was you."

"There's no secret about it now, I guess. I was so

worried about Maia getting taken by that fake movie producer. Anyway, I tried to talk to her when we ran into each other in the chocolate shop, but Aubrey Andrews Armstrong"—she spit the words out— "turned up, and I couldn't. So I went out to her house that evening."

She sighed. "I guess Lee told you I had run into him in California."

"She tried not to break any confidences," Joe said.

"Well, I guess my career, and maybe my marriage, are just about shot anyway. But, back to Tuesday. After I left the chocolate shop, I went back to the park to make sure the kids did the cleanup. It took more than an hour to pick up all the dirty paper napkins. But I was still worrying about Maia. So after I left the park, I went to her house to try to warn her about Armstrong."

"How did she take the news?"

"I didn't get to give it to her. Nobody answered the door."

"Oh. But Maia and Vernon's house is east of the Interstate. Why did you go over to the fruit stand?"

"What do you mean?"

"The fruit stand is on the west side of the Interstate. That's where Lee said she saw you."

"But I wasn't there."

"You just said you were at Maia and Vernon's."

"Yes, but I went back to the Interstate—from the east, just the way you'd expect—and I got on it headed north, and I went back to town."

"So you were never on the west side of the Interstate?"

"No." Maggie took a deep breath. "Does this mean that Lee *didn't* see me after all?"

"It might. She said that as she came out of the fruit stand she nearly ran into a red VW."

"A red one! I wasn't driving the red one! I had the new one. The acid green. Ken . . ."

She quit talking, but it was easy to finish her sentence.

It hadn't been Maggie I'd nearly run into as I drove out of the fruit stand. It had been Ken.

She promised to call the chief, and Joe hung up. We looked at each other.

"Why would either Maggie or Ken kill Silas Snow?" I said.

"Guessing by the weapon used—a shovel—it was a crime of passion. If one of them got really mad . . ."

"People don't get that mad at folks they don't know, Joe."

"True. We tend to murder those nearest and dearest to us."

"I hope that's not really true. But you've had a lot more experience with killers." In his previous life as an attorney, Joe had been a public defender. I knew he had defended accused killers.

"That was just a wisecrack, of course, Lee. Most people never have a reason to kill anybody. But anybody could be pushed over the edge, I guess."

"How?"

"It has to be something that they perceive as a real threat—either to their physical being, as killing in self-defense; to their property, like killing a burglar; or to their . . . I guess you could call it self-image. I guess killing your wife's lover would be a twisted form of that. Then there's revenge, getting even with somebody who harmed you or threatened your view of yourself."

"It's hard to fit any of those motives with either Maggie or Ken and Silas Snow. I don't think either of them had ever met Silas. They wouldn't have cared what he thought of them."

"Which probably means that they were out near the fruit stand for perfectly innocent reasons."

We were still mulling over the Ken, Maggie, and Silas relationship—or lack thereof—when the phone rang again. Aunt Nettie caught it downstairs, then called up to tell Joe it was for him.

"Probably Chief Jones," Joe said. He picked up the receiver.

I could hear the rush of profanity three feet away. "You *blankety-blank*! I'm going to come out there and mop the floor with you, you worthless piece of *excrement*! What do you mean? Telling my wife all that trash!"

CHOCOLATE CHAT

HALE AND HEART-Y

The good news about chocolate is—it's good for you.

Chocolate contains phenolic chemicals, the same chemicals behind red wine's well-documented ability to fight heart disease. Japanese research indicates that phenolics fight disases such as cancer and heart disease by increasing immune function and suppressing cell-damaging chemicals.

A 1.5-ounce chocolate bar contains as many phenolics as a five-ounce glass of cabernet. As might be expected, dark chocolate contains more phenolics than milk chocolate, and white chocolate contains very low levels.

But watch out! Chocolate may be healthful, but the fats and sugars mixed with it may counteract its value. For example, contrary to folklore, chocolate apparently does not promote tooth decay, higher cholesterol, acne, or hyperactivity. Alas, if you mix chocolate with *sugar,* all these things may result.

As for weighty matters: New products have been introduced over the past few years claiming to offer chocolate in low-sugar, low-fat, and low-carb versions. Just remember to read the labels carefully. "Low-sugar," "low-fat," and "low-carb" products are not always "low calorie."

Chapter 18

It wasn't Chief Hogan Jones, but I recognized the voice booming out the receiver and bouncing a yard away into my ear. It was Ken McNutt.

Nothing he said was very original; it was simply so surprising to hear that language and fury coming from the usually mild-mannered Ken. For the first time I *believed* he'd been a marine. Heck, judging from the words he used, I'd have believed he'd sailed with Captain Kidd.

Joe's reaction also surprised me. He didn't say a word. He didn't even seem to resent being cussed out.

He just listened until Ken ran down. When silence finally fell, he said, "Are you mad because I advised Maggie to go to Chief Jones or Lieutenant VanDam and tell one of them she was out near Silas Snow's fruit stand the night he was killed?"

The cursing broke out again. Joe held the phone at arm's length and waggled his eyebrows at me. He still seemed more amused than angry. When Ken again seemed to have run out of things to say, Joe spoke again. "I advise you to go talk to Jones or VanDam, too, Ken."

More swearing. This time the tirade didn't last as long, but it was still loud. Ken ended it with one statement I heard as clear as the call of a wood thrush on a Michigan summer night.

"I'm not going to let anybody hurt Maggie! I'll kill 'em first!"

"Nobody wants to hurt Maggie, Ken. But if she was out near the fruit stand, she may have seen something important."

"She wasn't near the fruit stand! She went to the Ensmingers house. And she didn't even see anybody there!"

For the first time Joe reacted to Ken's tirade. He snapped out an answer. "What did you say?"

"I said Maggie knows nothing about Silas Snow's death."

"No! No, you said—" Joe broke off. "Listen, Ken, this is vitally important. The fact that Maggie *didn't* see anybody. Has she told anybody else that?"

For the first time Ken spoke in an ordinary tone of voice. "What do you mean? She told you a few minutes ago."

"Yeah, and I didn't catch the importance of it until you repeated it. Maggie may be in danger because of what she *didn't* see. You've got to get her to a safe place."

"A safe place?" Ken sounded dazed.

"Yes. Are you at the school?"

"No. I'm at home. Maggie's at the school. She told me the number you called from."

"Call her and tell her to stay there. Go get her. Put Maggie on the floor of the backseat. Take her straight to the police station, around at the back. Make her run from the car to the station. Ask for VanDam. And stay there until you see him. Don't let her sit near a window."

There was a long silence. "Joe, I know I lost my temper. But you don't need to get even with me with some elaborate leg pull."

"Ken, this is no joke! Maggie could be in real danger. If you don't want to drive her to the station, I'll call VanDam and ask him to pick her up. Call her and tell her to stay away from windows until he gets there."

"No! No, I'll take her. But Joe, if you're kidding . . ."

"I am not kidding, Ken. This is exactly the piece of evidence VanDam and Hogan Jones have been looking for."

I was full of questions, of course, but Joe shook his head. He waved his hand at me, then punched numbers into the phone.

"Hogan," he said. "I just found out something." He quickly told the chief what Maggie had said. "I told Ken to get her to the station as fast as he can," he said. "You may be able to get enough for a warrant."

He gave a few more grunts of the "uh-huh" and "uh-uh" variety, then he hung up.

"I'd better get down to the station, meet Ken and Maggie," he said.

"Joe! What's going on?"

"I gotta go. You know enough to figure it out."

I followed him downstairs, still asking questions. Joe wasn't talking. He charged the back door, but Aunt Nettie and I wouldn't let him open it until we told him we couldn't take much more of my "disappearance."

"It's just too hard on people," I said. "My friends call up crying, and I feel like a louse."

Joe smiled. "I'll tell the chief. I think Maggie's evidence will allow him to bring in the killer. Maybe you can be found alive this evening."

He moved toward the door, then turned back. "I forgot to tell you one thing. I called the publisher of Maia's book."

"Oh? Did he pay her for it?"

"Yes and no. It seems that Vernon came to him and told him his wife's big ambition was to see the book in print. Vernon paid to have it published and even threw in an extra thousand so the publishers could offer her a small payment they called an 'advance.' Vernon even offered to pay more to ensure their silence, but the guy claims he didn't take the money."

I discovered I was furious. "That's the meanest thing I ever heard of."

"Meanest?"

"Yes. For Vernon to fool her that way, to let her think a publisher really wanted that awful book. It's a terrible thing to do."

"But if she really wanted to see it in print . . ."

I shook my head, but Aunt Nettie was the one who answered. "No, Joe. Vernon's motive might be good, but he fooled her. He wasn't honest. This has got to be kept secret. Not one of us can tell a soul. Not a soul. If the word gets out, Maia will be humiliated."

"I promise I won't tell anybody but Hogan. And I promise I'll never lie to either of you. Though I'm not smart enough to make either of you look foolish."

"I do a pretty good job of that for myself," I said.

Joe laughed, then gave me a kiss on the mouth and Aunt Nettie one on the cheek. He went out the kitchen door. Monte tried to go with him, but I caught him and kept him inside. Monte stood on his hind legs, scratching at the screen and whining as Joe drove away, traveling much faster than he usually did. He really seemed eager to meet Ken and Maggie. I still didn't understand why.

I looked after his truck. "I heard Maggie's story, too," I said. "I don't see anything to base an arrest on."

"What did she say?"

I repeated the story to Aunt Nettie.

"I don't see any special significance in it, either." Aunt Nettie sighed and gestured toward Monte, who was still scratching at the screen. "Monte's going to tear that screen up. I guess I'd better take him out again."

"I'll take a turn."

"No, Lee! You can't be seen."

"I won't be seen. I've been studying that map Hogan brought out. I can find a deserted road to walk on."

"You could skulk in the bushes, I guess, but somebody might come along."

"According to the map, I can go along the Baileys' drive and cut across to the Sheridans' cottage. Behind them I hit Mary Street, and that parallels Lake Shore Drive and goes clear down to One Hundred Eightieth Street. Every house on it is marked 'summer cottage.' There won't be a soul there."

"And that policeman sitting in our drive? What's he going to do when you stroll past him?"

"He's just here to keep reporters from coming in and asking rude questions. We're not prisoners."

She frowned, but I carried the day. After all, I wasn't confined to the house because I was safer there. As long as the rifleman thought I was dead in the woods, I was safe wherever I was. No, I had hidden out for nearly forty-eight hours so that Hogan Jones and Van-Dam could trick the killer of Silas Snow.

The wind was still blowing and the temperature was in the fifties, so I got a jacket. By then Monte was jumping around madly, realizing he was going out.

"He does need a longer walk," Aunt Nettie said. "I just took him around in the yard, since I had to stay within earshot of the telephone." She frowned. "Do you want me to come along? I don't want you to be nervous."

"Nervous about being in the woods? I may be, but I think it's better if I go out there and face the trees. It's a case of getting back on the horse that threw you."

"Be sure to come home before dark."

"It won't be dark for a couple of hours. I'm not going that far."

Monte and I started off. I didn't deliberately elude the cop in the driveway; I just happened to go out the back way, along the path to the Baileys' house, and he just happened not to see me.

Monte was a happy puppy. I tried telling him, "Walk," in a firm voice, but he knew I was no authority figure. He ran this way and that, yanking at his collar when he came to the end of the leash. I was glad I had the leash; he would have disappeared in a minute without it.

We walked alongside the Baileys' house—they were out of town—then went through their backyard and into the trees behind the house. A little path there led to the cottage of the Sheridans, their neighbors on the other side. That cottage was shuttered securely; the Sheridans wouldn't be back in Warner Pier until after Memorial Day.

Monte and I passed the Sheridans' cottage, then turned down their drive. It curved and exited on a sandy lane, which according to the map was named Mary Street. I had thought that road was just an extension of their drive.

Monte was doing fine, yipping at the occasional bird and sniffing at mysterious aromas he found in the bushes and trees that lined the lane. I acted much the same way, I guess. After the hours I'd spent closed up in an upstairs bedroom with blankets on the windows, it was good to be outside, breathing fresh air and feeling the exhilaration of brisk temperatures. I did my share of frisking around.

I was managing my phobia all right. The woods were threatening, true, but I didn't feel panicky. I felt liberated. Monte and I didn't hurry, we just strolled down that sand lane. Our easy pace allowed me to mull over Maggie's story as I went.

Gradually our surroundings changed. The woods on the left-hand side of the road cleared out. I could see a little sky on that side. We walked on, and the trees cleared more. We passed one final elm, and Monte and I found ourselves in an apple orchard—lots of short trees, but with plenty of space between them. I could see the sky.

I stopped and looked around. The elm I'd just passed, the apples—I was sure they were McIntosh. The scene was definitely familiar.

I spoke out loud. "Monte, this is Silas Snow's orchard. That elm is the one where the fruit ladder was propped. These are the apple trees Joe and I walked around to look at." I turned toward the west. "The Grundy cottage is beyond those bushes."

Monte cocked an ear at me, then scuttled ahead, trying to turn down the lane toward Lake Shore Drive, the lane Ken had come down in the red Volkswagen. I followed his tugging, and in a minute I saw the weather-beaten white siding of the cottage. We circled the little house as Monte snuffled around in the high weeds. When we got to the front porch, I sat down on the step, allowing Monte to scamper around at the end of his leash.

It was quiet, except for the wind in the trees. I could hear the lake surf, though it was much fainter than it had been the day I ran through the woods. Occasionally a bird called. Monte even sat still for a few minutes. It was the perfect place to continue mulling over Maggie's story. After all, Joe has said I could figure out what she *hadn't* seen that was so significant.

So I mulled. I began with the uncharacteristic reaction Ken had displayed when Joe urged Maggie to go to the police and tell them she had been near the fruit stand the night Silas Snow had been killed. Even though I had heard Ken's fury broadcasting through my very own telephone, it was hard to believe. What had caused him to go . . . well, berserk? And what had he said? "If anybody tries to hurt Maggie, I'll kill 'em."

Of course, Ken didn't mean it, I assured myself.

When Joe had listed off common motives for homicides, he hadn't listed that: protecting a loved one. Or would it be classified as part of a motive Joe had listed: protecting one's property?

But whatever his motivation, Ken had declared that he would kill to protect Maggie. How did that make her feel? Treasured? Or threatened?

Would Joe kill to protect me? Did I want him to? On the other hand, would I kill to protect Joe? I'd once tried to hit someone I thought was threatening him. Did that count?

Did all devoted married couples feel that way? Would Uncle Phil have killed to protect Aunt Nettie? Would Vernon kill to protect Maia?

I reminded myself that Vernon had spent several thousand dollars to make Maia's dearest wish come true, getting her novel into print. I might feel he'd been misguided, but he'd wanted to please her. Would he do more? Would he actually harm someone to protect her? I had no idea. In fact, my speculations were a silly way for me to spend my time.

Time. I held the leash in my hand and leaned back against the porch railing, almost dozing. Time.

The word reverberated out of my subconscious, and suddenly I was wide awake, with my adrenaline surging.

"Time! That's what Maggie's story does." I was so excited I spoke aloud. "She says she went by to try to see Maia after the drama club finished the cleanup at the park. And when she got to Maia and Vernon's, nobody was there!"

Maggie had left TenHuis Chocolade just after three o'clock. She said it took the kids more than an hour to clean up the park. So it would have been after four, but probably before five, when she started for the Ensmingers'. Nobody had answered her knock. But according to Maia and Vernon, they'd both been home at that time, taking showers and resting. They alibied each other.

"Monte," I said. "They lied. They're the two people with the strongest motives to kill Silas Snow, and they both lied about where they were when he was killed."

In my excitement, I had stood up. Monte was still snuffling along the cottage's foundation, checking out the weeds and saplings in case critters had left interesting smells along there. He was nearly to the corner of the cottage, close to the bathroom.

"Come on, Monte. We need to get back to Aunt Nettie's."

I guess I was still thinking about Maggie's destruction of Maia's and Vernon's alibis, because I forgot that Monte was fascinated with the bathroom. On our previous visit he'd tried to crawl under it.

The room sat on cement blocks and was barely attached to the main cottage. The dirt under it looked dark and crumbly. I could understand why Monte wanted to try get under there and practice his digging skills. But I didn't want Monte to carry that dirt back to Aunt Nettie's.

"No, Monte," I said. "Don't go under there!" I moved toward him, ready to pick him up.

But I had allowed the leash to develop some slack, and Monte took advantage of it. Like a flash he was under the bathroom, and a shower of soil came flying out as he began to dig.

"Monte! Stop that!" I tugged at his leash, but Monte wasn't budging. In fact, the dirt stopped flying out, and Monte's tail disappeared. I pulled at the leash again. I didn't want to yank too hard at his collar, but he wasn't taking a hint. I jerked. Still no result. In fact, there was no give to the leash at all. For a horrible moment I thought Monte had slipped his collar.

"Monte!" I dropped to my stomach in the weeds and looked under the bathroom.

To my annoyance I saw that the leash was looped around a cement block that was a central support for the bathroom. To my relief I saw that the other end was still attached to the puppy's collar.

"Monte! You naughty boy! Come out of there."

I was ignored, of course. In fact, unless Monte was a lot smarter than an ordinary dog, he wouldn't be able to figure out how to unwind his leash from the cement block.

I was going to have to crawl under there after him.

"Yuk!" I said. "Monte, I have a notion to leave you there."

That wasn't really an option. So I began to inch my way under, crawling through that nasty-looking dirt I hadn't wanted Monte to track into Aunt Nettie's house.

The bathroom sat between eighteen inches and two feet above the ground, so the crawl wasn't too tight. I had to keep my head down—not hard to remember when I pictured how many spiders were probably spinning webs on the bottom of the bathroom floor. I edged in. My sore elbows reminded me that I'd been doing this same sort of thing forty-eight hours earlier as I crawled through the bushes to get away from the rifleman. Luckily, I was wearing a jacket and some big Band-Aids to protect the scabs.

The bathroom wasn't large. My feet were still sticking out when I reached the cement block Monte had encircled with his leash. I tried to untangle the leash carefully. I didn't want to pull the cement block out of position. Doing that might mean a cast-iron, claw-foot bathtub or something just as heavy would come crashing through the floor and land on my head. So I reached around the block and took hold the leather strap close to Monte, then I tossed my end as far as I could and pulled gently.

In a minute I had all of the leash on one side of the cement block, and I was reeling Monte in, hand over hand, as if he were a fish. I wasn't too careful about not yanking on his collar. I wanted to get hold of him and get out of there.

Monte objected to being hauled out, naturally. He began to yip and pull away, but I said, "Come," firmly—as if that was going to make a difference. But like it or not, he did come. In a moment I was gripping his collar, and he was licking my face.

"Quit, Monte! If I get the giggles we'll never get out of here."

Miraculously, Monte did quit. He quit yapping, and he quit licking. His ears pricked up, and he twisted around, looking at something closer to the foundation of the house.

"What's the matter with you? Is something there?"

If there was something under that bathroom with Monte and me, I didn't want to know what it was. The most likely thing was a skunk. Even a woodchuck or a chipmunk could be bad. I began to scoot backward.

Then I heard the noise that Monte must have heard first.

It was a rapping noise. Regular. Rhythmic. It was not a wild animal noise. It was a human noise.

And six or eight feet away, in the foundation of the Grundy cottage, I saw a thin sliver of light.

Chapter 19

The next thing I saw, of course, was stars, because I jumped so high that I banged the back of my head on the underside of the bathroom floor.

Meanwhile I was wrestling Monte, who was sure there was something under that bathroom that he should be chewing on. He was alternately yapping and whining, and he definitely did not like being hauled up close to me and gripped. His clumsy puppy feet were still scrabbling madly, and he ignored my repeated shushes.

I could barely hear the tapping.

It was fairly loud. Tap, tap, tap. Then, slower. Tap. Tap. Tap. Then fast again. Tap, tap, tap. At the same time, the sliver of light grew brighter, then dimmer, then brighter again.

I couldn't pretend it was a skunk. There was a cellar of some sort under the Grundy cottage, and somebody was in there.

I tried to muzzle Monte with my hand. "Who's there?" My voice croaked.

"Help!" The answering voice was much louder

than I expected. I realized there was an opening in the cellar wall. Probably where there had once been a window. It had been blocked, but there was apparently nothing but a board between me and the person in the cellar. And there was a crack around the outside of the board.

"Who is it?" I repeated the words.

"Help! I've been kidnapped! Get me out!"

At that point Monte went absolutely wild. I don't know if he smelled a familiar smell or recognized a familiar voice. But I'll swear he knew who was in that cellar.

I called out again. "I'll get help! But who are you?"

"It's Aubrey! Aubrey Andrews Armstrong!"

I guess I'd already figured that out. Who else was missing around Warner Pier?

I began to scoot backward, coming out from under the bathroom and taking the protesting Monte with me. Aubrey began to bang on the board again.

"I'll try to get you out!" I yelled. The banging stopped.

I kept scooting until I was out from under the bathroom. My hair was full of spider webs and my clothes were covered with dirt, but I could stand up. I gave a shudder and hoped I wouldn't have to go under anything like that bathroom ever again. Then I began to try to figure out how to get into the cellar.

I made a quick circuit of the house, but couldn't find an entrance. I didn't find another cellar window, or even a former window. If such an opening existed, it was under the little front sleeping porch. That was even closer to the ground than the bathroom, and I definitely wasn't interested in crawling under there.

No, the cellar must be entered only from inside the cottage. I'd have to break into the house.

There was a back door, but no back step or porch; the solid wooden door opened directly onto the grass. And when I examined it, the grass was crushed. Someone had been walking on that grass. Apparently that was the way Aubrey's kidnapper had gone in and out of the cottage.

I tried the door. It was locked, of course. I looked around for a rock or a stick I could use to smash it open.

Monte was driving me crazy, tugging at his leash and barking. I looped his leash around one of the saplings growing in the yard, one far enough from the bathroom that he couldn't crawl under again. I tied the leash securely. Then I felt in my pocket and found a handful of doggy treats I'd brought along. One of them kept him quiet for a moment.

I picked up a dead limb at the back of the yard. I used it to whack at the door a couple of times, but all it did was chip the paint. That wasn't going to work. I'd have to get in through a window. I carried the dead limb around the house, looking for a window that would be easy to climb through, once I either got it open or smashed through the glass.

And as I walked my brain belatedly began to work.

It occurred to me that the guy in the cellar wasn't just any guy. He was Aubrey Andrews Armstrong. Despite his charming personality, Aubrey was a bad guy. He was a crook who had, or so I was convinced, tried to con my Aunt Nettie. He had tried to blackmail Maggie, one of my best friends. He had conned Maia—who might be a foolish woman, but who didn't deserve to be tricked—by telling her he was going to make a movie of her book. He had enticed high school kids like Tracy with visions of movie stardom.

I wasn't afraid of Aubrey, but maybe I should be. After all, he had barely appeared on the scene when Silas Snow was killed. Maybe he *was* involved in that, in spite of his alibi.

True, if Vernon and Maia had lied about being home at the time Silas was killed, it looked as if the two of them were the most likely culprits. But Maia was closely hooked up with Aubrey; he might be her accomplice.

Letting Aubrey out of that cellar might be the dumbest thing I ever did in my life. It might even be the last thing I ever did in my life.

I decided Aubrey could stay in his cellar a little longer. I tossed my dead branch aside. Then I went back to the bathroom, lay down on my stomach, and called out. "Aubrey!"

"Get me out of here!"

"I can't get into the house! I'll have to go for help!"

"No! No! It's nearly five o'clock! He'll be back!"

"Who?"

"Vernon! He locked me down here."

Vernon? I didn't have time to analyze the situation thoroughly, but Vernon was definitely on the list of possibles for Silas's killer.

But why had he kidnapped Aubrey?

I had no idea. Not that Vernon wouldn't make an ideal kidnapper. He was so dependable. Aubrey would trust him, just as I would have. If Vernon came by my house at three a.m. and said, "Let's go for a ride," I'd get right in his pickup. And if Vernon were going to kidnap somebody, the Grundy cottage would be a logical place for him to keep his captive imprisoned. Vernon was in charge of the Snow property, at least for the moment, and he could well be familiar with the cottage and its facilities—such as a cellar none of the rest of us had realized was there. And the Grundy cottage was remote from year-round houses. Unless some of the high school kids decided to go treasure hunting, no one was likely to come by.

Yes, I could picture Vernon as a kidnapper.

Aubrey started banging on the board again.

I yelled. "I'll hurry!"

Then I jumped to my feet, moved to the sapling where I'd tied Monte, and began to loosen his leash.

I was still on my knees when I heard a motor.

It sounded powerful. Could it be a truck? I couldn't see it, but it seemed to be pulling into the Grundy cottage. I froze as the sound stopped. Then I heard a door open. It was right on the other side of the cottage.

It had to be Vernon. He was there to check on Aubrey. And he'd been entering the cottage by its back door, a door that wasn't ten feet from me.

The leash came loose, and I grabbed it. Then I scooped up Monte and ran for the nearest hiding place—under that darn bathroom. I dropped to my stomach and, moving sideways, I scrunched back in among the spiders and dirt.

My life depended on Monte. If he made a noise, Vernon might haul me out, and if Vernon was really a killer, he might then beat my head in.

I pulled the little dog close to me. Then I took another doggy treat from my jacket pocket and gave it to him. I understood the danger, but Monte was only a baby animal. If he barked, yipped, or whined, I'd be killed.

I cuddled him and stroked his chocolate fur, each motion a prayer. Beyond him I saw heavy farmer's boots come around the corner of the cottage. A picnic cooler, the kind with a top that swings open, was placed on the grass. I heard sounds of metal on metal, then the back door of the cottage swung in. A large, strong hand reached down and picked up the cooler. Vernon—I couldn't see his face, but I didn't doubt it was him—went inside.

I gave him a moment, listening to the noises from inside the cottage; then I gave Monte another doggy treat to keep him quiet, and I crawled out from under the bathroom. I got to my feet, scooped the dog up, and tiptoed across the yard, headed for home, telephone, and police.

That was my intention, anyway. But the back door to the cottage was standing open. I hoped that Vernon was down in the cellar with Aubrey, but I didn't dare pass that open door. I stopped and looked through the crack between the door and the jamb.

The door opened into the little kitchen area of the cottage. I could see glimpses of the apartment-sized range, the tiny refrigerator, and the back of the small counter that separated kitchen area from living room. Right in the middle of the kitchen floor was a trapdoor, fastened down with a padlock.

And kneeling on the floor beside it was Vernon.

I nearly died. We weren't three feet apart.

Luckily, Vernon was looking down, fooling with the padlock. I jumped back and stood beside the door, with my back against the wall. If Vernon turned around or put his head out the door . . . well, I might be able to outrun him.

Unless he had his rifle handy.

I decided passing the open door was too risky. I'd have to circle around the house.

I edged to my right, giving Monte another dog yummy, passed the bathroom, and went along the south side of the cottage, keeping as quiet as possible. I reached the corner by the disheveled porch and started to cross in front of the cottage.

Then I saw movement through the trees.

Immediately I jumped back, behind the solid wall of the south side of the cottage. I knelt and peeked around the corner. In that position my head was behind the old rusty cot frame in the corner of the sleeping porch. I hoped I'd be able to see if someone was coming. I squinted my eyes, trying to locate the movement I'd seen.

It wasn't hard. I'd barely poked my head around the corner when the bushes between the cottage and Lake Shore Drive parted.

Maia stepped out.

My first thought was that she must have come to rescue Aubrey. She was such a fan of his. Maybe she had figured out that Vernon was holding him prisoner and had come to let him out.

Then I noticed Maia was holding a rifle across her chest. Maybe she hadn't come to let Aubrey out. Maybe she'd come to kill him.

I'm no expert on firearms, but my father is a deer hunter, and he tried to get me interested in the sport. The rifle Maia was carrying would have been right at home in a Texas deer camp. It had a long barrel. It had a scope. I could see the bolt used to cock it.

Maia was marching along, holding the rifle with its barrel pointed upward, as if she were making a training video on hunting safety. She was smiling a little. Her eyes were fixed. She walked between the cottage and Vernon's truck, which he'd parked in the drive, and disappeared from sight.

Now how was I going to get home? If I went around the back, past the back door, Vernon might look out and see me. If I went around the front, I might run into Maia. If I went through the bushes to get to Lake Shore Drive, I'd be crashing around, and one of them would hear me.

I decided I had to cross in front of the house and peek around the corner. Maybe Maia had followed Vernon to the back door. She'd been marching forward so purposefully that I doubted she'd notice me unless I punched her between the shoulder blades.

So, feeding Monte another treat, I crossed in front of the cottage and peeked around the corner. No Maia. She'd apparently gone around the corner and was behind the house. I started to slip around on the other side of Vernon's truck. I could hide behind it and get to Mary Street.

This would have been a good plan, if there hadn't been a window in the cottage. Somehow I'd forgotten that, and I crossed right in front of it.

It was a miracle that neither of them saw me. But I saw what was going on inside, and I was so startled I stopped in my tracks and looked into the cottage.

I didn't see Maia. What I saw was Vernon. He was kneeling on the kitchen floor, right where he'd been when I saw him a few seconds earlier, but he'd turned to face the door. He was holding his arms up as high as his head. He had his back to me, because he was looking out the back door.

Then I saw the rifle barrel.

It was pointed through the back door. Right at Vernon. Maia was holding her husband at gunpoint.

I couldn't see her, but the cottage was small. I could hear Maia's voice. She was speaking calmly and rationally.

"Don't you see, Vernon? I had to kill Uncle Silas. He was going to lie, to tell everyone that my grandmother—my very own grandmother!—killed Dennis Grundy. I'm so sorry you interfered. Now I'm going to have to kill you."

Maia was going to kill Vernon. And maybe Aubrey.

What could I do?

Before I could figure out the answer to that one, it was too late to think about it. I guess I got so scared I lost muscle control. I didn't faint, scream, or wet my pants. I did something worse.

I dropped Monte.

Barking joyously, he ran for the corner of the cottage, eager to get back under that darn bathroom, where he could dig and yap at his master.

I jumped for the trailing leash, then realized I'd

better let the dog go. I needed to get out of there. I probably should have run for Lake Shore Drive, but I was facing toward Mary Street, so I ran that way. As I passed the corner of the cottage, I heard a man's voice, roaring. And I heard a scream.

I looked right, ready to duck a rifle shot—as if I could—and I saw Vernon sprawled on top of Maia. They were struggling for the rifle. Maia still had it, but Vernon was trying to take it away from her. And somehow Monte and his leash were part of the mix.

I didn't consciously change my route, but the next thing I knew I'd joined the fray. I was kicking at Maia's hand. Then I grabbed the butt of the rifle and yanked.

Maia was screaming, Vernon was growling, Monte was barking madly, and, from inside the cellar, Aubrey was yelling for help.

Suddenly the rifle went off. The kick made Maia lose her grip, but I still had hold of the butt. I flew backward and landed on my rear end. But I had the rifle.

Vernon was still trying to pin Maia down. Neither of them seemed to be bleeding, and I didn't think I'd been shot, either.

I scrambled to my feet and looked at the rifle. I fought the impulse to throw it into the bushes.

Instead I yelled. "Stop fighting!" Then I threw back the bolt and cocked the rifle.

That noise got their attention. Both Maia and Vernon stopped moving, though Maia had begun to sob.

"Maia's not the only person with deer hunters in her family," I said. "I know how to use this thing."

Maia sobbed. "But you're dead!" she said. "I tried so hard to kill you. The police said you had disappeared."

"I'm back," I said. "And you'd better not move a muscle."

It took me a few seconds to figure out what I wanted them to do. After all, we were in a deserted spot. Even firing off a rifle was not guaranteed to bring the cops running. I had two prisoners—three if you counted Aubrey. What was I going to do with them? March down the road to Aunt Nettie's? That didn't seem like a sensible idea. Finally I figured out a simple plan.

"Vernon," I said. "Dump Maia down in that cellar with Aubrey."

Both of them were tangled in Monte's leash, so it wasn't easy. Maia fought and screamed, but Vernon finally managed to get her into the cellar. He'd removed any stairs or ladder that had once been there, so he just dropped her over the edge. Then he turned to me. He looked relieved. "That'll keep her safe for the moment."

I still had the rifle pointed at him. "Now you. Into the cellar."

"But, Lee, I didn't kill anybody! I just penned Aubrey up to keep Maia from killing him!"

"I don't care why you did it. Get down there."

He still hesitated, and I spoke again. "If you leave them down there alone, they'll kill each other."

He grimaced, knelt and slid into the cellar feet first. Just before his head disappeared, I spoke again. "Wait! Where's the padlock? And the key?"

"They're on the counter."

Monte had been whining, wanting to go down in the cellar and join his master. Luckily, he was afraid to jump that far. I was able to scoop him up, swing the trapdoor shut, and lock it. I hid the rifle under the porch.

Then I ran for Aunt Nettie's, still holding Monte in my arms.

I pounded along, down the overgrown road that led to Silas's apple orchard. Then I turned onto Mary

Street and began to run down the sandy lane. I felt as if I was home free.

Until I rounded a curve, and I collided with a tree trunk.

At least that's what it seemed like at the moment. I ran right into a tall, thin, hard thing that loomed up right in the middle of the road.

The tall thing and I were lying in a heap before I realized I had run headlong into Joe.

I dropped the dog and threw my arms around Joe's neck. "Everyone's gone besieged! I mean, berserk! I locked them up!"

But Joe wasn't listening to me. He was talking. "Lee! Lee! If anyone's done anything to hurt you, I'll kill 'em! I couldn't go on living without you!"

Chapter 20

Then we spoke—or maybe we yelled incoherently—at the same time. I said, "Where did you come from?" Joe said, "Did you tangle with Maia?"

"I tangled with Maia! With Vernon! And with Aubrey! With every nut on the lakeshore!"

"You found Aubrey? Hogan was sure he was dead."

"He wasn't a minute ago, but he may be now. He's locked in the cellar of the Grundy cottage with Maia and Vernon."

"You're kidding! How did that happen?"

"It was the only way I could think of to make the three of them stay put. What are you doing here?"

"Looking for you. We heard the shots. Nettie's calling the cops."

Then he kissed me. Not passionately. Tenderly. He pulled me really close, which is an awkward thing to do when you're both sitting in the middle of a sandy road and there's a big puppy involved. But he managed it. And when he spoke again, he'd stopped yelling. He whispered. "Lee. If anything happened to you—I just couldn't go on. When I heard those rifle shots, I thought my heart had stopped beating. I didn't see how you could escape that crazy woman with a rifle twice. If you don't marry me, I may . . . I don't know what I'll do."

It was the most romantic thing anybody ever said to me. Joe didn't want to get married. He wanted to marry me.

We might have sat in the dirt, snuggling, for a long time, but Monte decided he needed attention. He wiggled in between us, put his front paws on Joe's shoulders, and began to lick his face. We both laughed, and we were getting to our feet when I heard footsteps, coming fast. It was, of course, Aunt Nettie. She hugged my neck. The tears in her eyes told me how relieved she was to see me alive and unhurt.

"I'll go to the Grundy cottage and wait for the chief," Joe said. "You two go back to the house."

"The rifle's under the bathroom," I said.

"How did it get *there*?"

"I wanted to hide it after I locked everybody in the cellar."

Joe closed his eyes and shook his head. "Let's not go into it. You'll have to make a statement later." Then he kissed me on the cheek. "I'll just have to remember that Texas gals can be pretty fierce. They can face down three villains armed with rifles and come out on top."

He trotted off down the road toward the Grundy cottage. Aunt Nettie and I went back to her house, and I took a shower and washed my hair. It took two washes and three rinses before I felt spider-free.

Aunt Nettie kept stalling about dinner. It was eight o'clock, and I was getting pretty hungry when Joe and Chief Jones showed up, and I realized why she'd been waiting.

The chief came in the dining room, put his hands on his hips, stared at me, and shook his head slowly. "Lee, what are you? Some kind of vigilante? Vernon says you grabbed that rifle away from Maia and threw the two of them down in that cellar without even letting go of the pup."

"Actually, the puppy accomplished it all. He distracted Maia. That let Vernon jump her. Then Monte wound both of them up in his leash. I didn't try to grab the rifle until he had them subdued."

"That's not the way Vernon tells it."

"Maybe Monte and I worked as a team. But is what Maia said true? Did she kill her uncle?"

"She's saying she did," Hogan said.

Aunt Nettie interrupted to insist that Joe and Hogan join us for dinner. It wasn't too hard for her to persuade them; especially when she said she'd hoped they'd come by, so she'd cooked enough for four. "And don't explain anything until I come," she said. "Just make small talk."

Ten minutes later she had a platter of bratwurst and sauerkraut on the table, along with carrot and raisin salad and two kinds of bread from the good bakery. "You'll have to talk and eat at the same time," Aunt Nettie said. "Lee and I have a lot of questions."

I asked the first one. "Hogan, is Maia explaining why she killed Silas Snow?"

"Not very clearly. Something about her grandmother. Since her grandmother's been dead since the 1930s, that's hard to understand."

"Was her grandmother the mother of Julia Snow? Or the wicked stepmother, the one in the book?"

Aunt Nettie answered. "I've been asking the ladies in the shop," she said. "She was the stepmother. Julia's father—I think his name was William Snow—had been left a widower with the one daughter, Julia. I guess he sort of let her grow up on her own. Finally, when Julia was fourteen, he married again. The second wife, Ellen, was only eighteen. Naturally, she and Julia didn't get along. She had a new baby the first year she and William were married. That was Maia's mother. Ellen had another baby the year after Julia ran off. Silas. But her health wasn't good. She went over to Jackson and stayed with relatives while she was pregnant. And she died, or so they said, when Silas was born. Silas and Maia's mother were raised by William's sister.''

The chief stopped with his fork in the air. "Did you say, 'Or so they said?' Didn't the ladies in the shop think this second Mrs. Snow really died?"

Aunt Nettie sighed. "Hazel asked her mother, who's way over ninety but sharp as a tack. And she said that the stepmother was sort of nutty. She hadn't mentioned being pregnant again to anybody in the neighborhood. And she left the first baby behind; William's sister came to take care of her. At the time, there was some gossip about the new baby, Silas. Some people thought he looked a lot more like Julia than like the stepmother."

I gasped. "That fits right in with what Dolly told us. Julia told Dolly that 'her family' killed her lover. She blamed her father, I'm sure. But if it had really been her stepmother . . . Well, there's a situation."

Joe shook his head. "If the two women—both of them just teenagers—had been rivals not only in the household, but also for the affections of this gangster-type, they certainly had the makings of a hot situation."

"Darn," I said. "Maybe it *would* make a good movie."

We all thought that over, then Aunt Nettie went on. "Dolly's grandmother, Julia Snow, told Dolly her baby by Dennis Grundy had been adopted. But her father could have arranged to take the baby himself."

Hogan shook his head. "That would make Silas

the son of Julia Snow and Dennis Grundy. Hard to believe."

"And who knows what happened to the stepmother, Ellen," I said. "Even if William wasn't willing to turn her in for murder, he may have thrown her out. If he didn't kill Dennis Grundy himself."

"We'll never figure all that out," Hogan said. "It's been too long. But I can see that, if Silas told Maia a story so different from what she'd written—well, she was none too stable to begin with. She might have thought it would ruin the chances that her book would be the basis of a movie. It could well have pushed her over the edge. And she picked up the shovel."

I shuddered. "But how did Vernon get involved?"

"His story is that he found Maia standing over her uncle's body. He got her home, then made her take a long shower. He told her to say that they'd been together at the house from four o'clock until Aubrey and Nettie came to pick them up at seven."

"But Maggie had come by their house."

"Right. Actually, they could have claimed they didn't hear the doorbell for the shower. Or some other reason. We wouldn't have been able to disprove it. But Maia's too nutty to cover up anymore, and Vernon's—well, resigned is the best word, I guess. He did all he could to protect her."

Joe spoke then. "Actually, Vernon claims he was simply trying to keep her from killing anybody else until he could get her committed."

The chief made a growling noise. "Not that that would have kept us from charging her. But he thought it would."

I remembered how Vernon had sobbed after I told him Aubrey was probably a con man. To realize that Maia had killed her uncle because she had a false idea her book was going to be made into a movie would have been hard to take. That raised another question, and I asked it. "Why did Maia try to kill Aubrey?"

"Because Vernon told her it looked like he was a crook. Then he mentioned he'd told Armstrong he could go over to the Grundy cottage. Next thing he knew, or so he claims, Maia had slipped out of the house and her deer rifle was gone. When he heard that somebody had taken a shot at Aubrey, he didn't know just what to do."

"He tried to drug her," I said. Joe and Hogan both stared at me, openmouthed, but Aunt Nettie nodded.

We told them about going out to Ensminger house on a condolence call and finding that Maia was out and Vernon wanted to know why she hadn't taken her medicine. Then, when I went back a day later, Maia was none too coherent. "I guess when Vernon couldn't keep Maia at home, he kidnapped Aubrey to keep him out of her way," I said.

"That's his story, anyway." Hogan shrugged. "I'll leave the charges up to the prosecutors."

Hogan took a big bite of bratwurst, and Aunt Nettie spoke. "But why did Maia try to kill Lee?"

Hogan nodded toward Joe, and Joe took up the tale. "That first time we went to the Grundy cottage, Lee and I walked back into the orchard. We noticed a fruit ladder by a big maple tree. But right about then, you and Aubrey called out that you were ready to go, so we turned around and went back. What Lee and I didn't notice was that Maia was up in that tree."

"What!" I gasped. "And we didn't see her?"

"No, the leaves were thick. But as near as the lab guys can tell from the angle of the shot that hit Aubrey's van, the rifle was fired from up in that tree." Joe gestured with his fork. "Lee, when you went out to the Ensminger place and saw Maia, did you mention that tree?"

"Not that I can remember. I asked Vernon some

questions about orchards. Maybe I mentioned ladders. Or something."

"Whatever you said, Maia interpreted it as a threat. She decided to lure you out to the lonely end of Inland Road and take care of the situation."

Aunt Nettie suddenly dabbed at her eyes with her napkin, then left the table. I started to go after her, but Hogan waved me back into my chair.

"Let me," he said. "I've had a lot of experience with tearful ladies."

Joe and I stared at our plates. Then he reached over and squeezed my hand.

"Don't say anything," I said. "You don't want two weeping women on your hands."

He grinned. "Maybe you'd like to know what Ken was doing hanging around Snow's place."

"What?"

"Looking for property. He thought Silas might sell him an acre or so, maybe even the Grundy cottage. He and Maggie had talked about building a house."

"I thought they were interested in buying Lindy and Tony's house and remodeling."

"They were. They are still, I guess."

"But Maggie called Lindy and told her they might be leaving Warner Pier."

"That was when Maggie thought Aubrey was going to tell whatever it is she doesn't want told. She thought she was going to lose her job over it. But she and Ken weren't communicating very well. He got the idea she wanted to build a house from scratch, maybe in a more rural area. So he tried to approach Silas about buying a lot."

"What a mix-up."

Aunt Nettie and Hogan came back to the table then. Apparently Hogan had had the right formula for cheering her up; Aunt Nettie looked pink and smiley.

"Okay," I said. "When is Aubrey going to come and get his dog?"

Joe and Hogan cleared their throats and looked all around the room. Even Aunt Nettie changed her expression from happy to slightly guilty. "Oh, dear," she said. "Hogan, you simply have to tell Lee what's going on."

"Don't tell me," I said. "We're stuck with Monte."

Hogan laughed. "You are for a few days at least. I'm holding Aubrey for Wisconsin authorities."

"What! What did he do?"

"They allege he ran a con in a small town, claiming he was going to make a movie there and looking for local investors. I got a notice about it a couple of weeks ago on a little e-mail news list I follow."

"So you knew he as a crook the minute he showed up! And you let Aunt Nettie get involved with him!"

Aunt Nettie giggled. "Actually, I was encouraged to get involved with him."

"Hogan!" I was scandalized.

"Lee, I couldn't hold him without a warrant. And if he left Warner Pier the Wisconsin police would have to wait until he showed up someplace else. I thought if we made it look as if there was a strong possibility that a well-to-do businesswoman such as your aunt was interested in his project, he'd hang around. I didn't think it would take more than forty-eight hours to settle the whole thing."

He reached over and squeezed Aunt Nettie's hand. "I will admit I didn't anticipate his actually taking her out. But he didn't have any history of violence, and Nettie had the sense never to be alone with him for more than a few minutes."

Aunt Nettie laughed. "Just call me Undercover Auntie!"

"Why didn't you tell me?" I said.

"Well," Hogan said, "you were so scandalized at the thought of your aunt going out on a date . . ."

"Not on a date! On a date with a strange man I found very suspicious!"

Hogan nodded. "And you were right to be suspicious, Lee. You rumbled Aubrey Andrews Armstrong right away. And so did Joe. He barely met the guy, and he came running to me about him."

Joe nodded. "Hogan recognized the description, including the dog, right away, and we decided to keep quiet until he could find out where Armstrong was wanted."

"But what about the other people in Warner Pier he cheated? Like Sarajane, at the B&B?"

"I think there's enough money in the Victim's Compensation Fund to satisfy Armstrong's local debts."

"Good. But that leaves my first question unanswered. What about Monte? Do Aunt Nettie and I have to build a fence and enroll in obedience classes?"

"That I can't answer," Hogan said. "Monte still belongs to Armstrong. He'll have to decide what to do about him. Since a purebred dog is worth quite a bit of money, Monte may be for sale."

I found out a few more things over the next few days.

The antique money, Hogan learned, had been planted by Maia, as Aubrey and Joe had suspected. She apparently thought this would make her novel seem more authentic and attractive to a moviemaker.

Aubrey Andrews Armstrong's business card—the one I'd been looking for when I discovered the body of Silas Snow—had turned up in the trash can at the fruit stand. I'd never thought to ask Hogan if it had been found.

The director of the Michigan Film Office e-mailed on the next Monday, telling me and Chuck O'Riley that a fake movie producer had been making the rounds of the upper Midwest and that we should contact law enforcement officials.

Maggie never offered to tell any of us what threat Aubrey had used to blackmail her. I think, however, that she did tell Ken. He's just as protective of her as ever. And they did buy Lindy and Tony's house.

Little Tony Herrera, ten-year-old son of my pal Lindy, listened to his parents talking about the case and got the idea that Monte was going to have to go to jail with his master. He cried all night. When his grandfather, Warner Pier mayor Mike Herrera, heard about this, he drove to the Warner County Jail and made Aubrey Andrews Armstrong a cash offer for the dog. Aubrey, who definitely needed money at that moment, agreed to sell. He did make Mike promise that Tony and Monte would enroll in obedience training. So Monte now lives with Tony, Lindy, Little Tony, Marcia, Alicia, and Pinto in the Vandermeer house—with a bedroom for each kid and a big backyard. Pinto still rules that backyard.

The most surprising outcome was revealed after Joe and Hogan left on the night the arrests were made. Aunt Nettie and I stood on the front porch to wave both of them off. Then she turned and gave me a big hug.

"I'm all right now," I said. "You don't need to worry."

"I'm not worried! I'm excited!"

"What about?"

"Lee! Hogan asked me to go out to dinner with him!"

I squealed. Aunt Nettie squealed. We hopped around like sixteen-year-olds planning for the junior prom.

"That's wonderful!" I said. "He's the catch of Warner Pier. You'll be the envy of all your friends."

"Yes." Aunt Nettie smiled her sweetest smile. "But that's not why I want to go."

As for Joe and me—well, I advised him to go with

the white tile for the bathroom in his new apartment. Then he could put up a patterned wallpaper. And, yes, I went along to help pick out the wallpaper.

The wedding's set for May.

Read on for a preview of JoAnna Carl's
next mouthwatering Chocoholic Mystery
featuring charming sleuth Lee McKinney

The Chocolate
Mouse Mystery

Available in Fall 2005 from Signet

"I'm sick and tired of deleting this stupid inspirational junk," I said. "If Julie Singletree doesn't stop sending it, I'm going to kill her, as well as her messages."

I'd been talking to myself, but when I raised my eyes from the computer screen, I realized I was also snarling at Aunt Nettie. She had nothing to do with the e-mail that had been driving me crazy, but she had innocently walked into my office, making herself a handy target for a glare.

Aunt Nettie smiled placidly; she'd understood that I was mad at my e-mail, not her. "Are you talking about that silly girl who's a party planner?"

"Yes. I know she got us that big order for the chocolate mice, but I'm beginning to think the business she could throw our way can't be worth the nausea brought on by these daily doses of Victorian sentiment."

Aunt Nettie settled her solid Dutch figure into a chair and adjusted the white food-service hairnet that covered her hair—blond, streaked with gray. I don't know how she works with chocolate all day long and keeps her white tunic and pants so sparkling clean.

"Victorian sentiment certainly isn't your style, Lee," she said.

"Julie is sending five of us half a dozen messages every day, and I am not interested in her childish hearts-and-flowers view of life. She alternates between ain't-life-grand and ain't-like-a-bitch, but both versions are coated with silly sugar. She never has anything clever or witty. Just dumb."

"Why haven't you asked to be taken off her list?"

I sighed and reached into my top desk drawer to raid my stash of Bailey's Irish Cream bonbons. ("Classic cream liqueur interior in dark chocolate.") Nothing soothes the troubled mind like a dose of chocolate.

"I suppose I kept thinking that if I didn't respond she'd simply drop me from her jokes-and-junk list," I said.

"You didn't even want to tell her you don't want to receive any more spam?"

"Oh, it's not spam. She'd made up a little list of us—it's all west Michigan people connected with the fine foods and parties trade. Lindy's on it, thanks to her new job in catering. There's Jason Foster—he has a restaurant in Saugatuck. There's Carolyn Rose at Warner Pier Floral. Margaret Van Meter, the cake decorating gal. And the Denhams at Hideaway Inn."

I gestured toward the screen. "This message is typical. 'A Prayer for the Working Woman.' I haven't read it, but I already know what it says."

"What?" Aunt Nettie smiled. "Since I've worked all my life, I might benefit from a little prayer."

"I can make you a printout, if you can stand the grossly lush roses Julie uses as a border." I punched the appropriate keys as I talked. "I predict it will be about how downtrodden women are today because most of us work."

"You'll have to assert yourself, Lee. Tell her you don't like her e-mails."

I sighed. "About the time I tell her that, she'll land a big wedding, and the bride will want enough bon-bons and truffles for four hundred people, and we'll lose out on a couple of thousand dollars in business. Or Schrader Laboratories will plan another banquet and want an additional three hundred souvenir boxes of mice."

I gestured toward the decorated gift box on the corner of my desk. Aunt Nettie had shipped off the whole order two weeks before, but I'd saved one as a sample. The box contained a dozen one-inch choco-late mice—six replicas of laboratory mice in white chocolate and six tiny versions of a computer mouse, half in milk chocolate and half in dark.

Schrader Laboratories is a Grand Rapids firm that does product testing—sometimes using laboratory mice and sometimes computers. A special item like the souvenir made for their annual dinner meant risk-free profit for TenHuis Chocolade; we know they're sold before we order the boxes they'll be packed in.

"That was a nice bit of business Julie threw our way, even if she did get the order from a relative," I said. "I can put up with a certain amount of gooey sentiment for that amount of money."

"It might be cheaper to give it up than to hire a psychiatrist. You've got plenty to do. Tell Julie your mean old boss has cracked down on nonbusiness e-mail."

Aunt Nettie smiled her usual sweet smile. "And I really am going to add to your chores. We need Amaretto."

"I'll get some on my way home."

Amaretto is used to flavor a truffle that is ex-tremely popular with our customers. Its mainly white color makes it an ideal accent for boxes of Valentine candy and at that moment we were just two weeks away from Valentine's Day. I knew Aunt Nettie and the twenty-five ladies who actually make TenHuis chocolates had been using a lot of Amaretto as they got ready for the major chocolate holiday. But liqueurs go a long way when used only for flavoring; one bottle would probably see us through the rush.

I handed Aunt Nettie the printout of Julie's dumb e-mail, all six pages of it. Julie never cleans the previous messages off the bottom of e-mails she forwards or replies to. Then Aunt Nettie went back to her antiseptically clean workroom.

I wrote "Amaretto" on a Post-it and stuck the note to the side of my handbag before I turned back to my computer. I manipulated my mouse until the arrow was on "Reply All" and clicked it. Then I stared at the screen, trying to figure out how to be tactful and still stop Julie's daily drivel.

"Dear Group," I typed. Maybe Julie wouldn't feel that I'd singled her out. "This is one of the busiest seasons for the chocolate business, and my aunt and I have decided we simply have to crack down on nonbusiness e-mail. As you know, at least half our orders come in by e-mail, so I spend a lot of time clearing it. As great as the jokes and inspirational material that we exchange on this list can be," I lied, "I just can't justify the time I spend reading them. So please drop me from the joke/inspiration list. But please continue to include me in the business tips!"

I sent the message to the whole list, feeling smug. I was genuinely hopeful that I'd managed to drop the cornball philosophy without dropping some valuable business associates along with it.

I wasn't prepared the next day when I got a call from Lindy Herrera, my best friend and a manager for Herrera Catering.

"Lee!" Lindy sounded frantic. "Have you had the television on?"

"No, why?"

"I was watching the early morning news— Oh, Lee, it's awful!"

"What's happened?"

"It's Julie Singletree! She's been murdered!"

About the Author

JoAnna Carl is the pseudonym of a multipublished mystery writer. She spent more than twenty-five years in the newspaper business, working as a reporter, feature writer, editor, and columnist. She holds a degree in journalism from the University of Oklahoma and also studied in the O.U. Professional Writing Program. She lives in Oklahoma, but spends much of each summer at a cottage on Lake Michigan near several communities similar to the fictional town of Warner Pier. She and her husband of forty-plus years have three children and three grandchildren. As a writer, she shamelessly exploits the skills of her children: one daughter who works for a chocolate maker, another daughter who is a CPA, and a son who is a librarian. She may be reached through her Web site at www.joannacarl.com.